Slipknot

Slipknot

PRISCILLA MASTERS

First published in Great Britain in 2007 by
Allison & Busby Limited
13 Charlotte Mews
London W1T 4EJ
www.allisonandbusby.com

Copyright © 2007 by PRISCILLA MASTERS

The moral right of the author has been asserted.

A CIP catalogue record for this book is available from
the British Library.

10 9 8 7 6 5 4 3 2 1

ISBN 0 7490 8174 0
978-0-7490-8174-4

Typeset in 11/16 pt Sabon by
Terry Shannon

Printed and bound in Wales by
Creative Print and Design, Ebbw Vale

Born in Yorkshire and brought up in south Wales, PRISCILLA MASTERS is the author of the popular series set in the Staffordshire moorlands featuring Detective Inspector Joanna Piercy. She has also written four medical standalone mysteries.

Slipknot is the second in the series featuring coroner Martha Gunn, set in the medieval town of Shrewsbury. Masters has two sons and lives in Staffordshire. She works part time as a nurse.

INTRODUCTION

The second in the Martha Gunn series, set in the medieval town of Shrewsbury, *Slipknot* explores the theme of mothers and sons being parted and the futility of young lives wasted. While Coroner Gunn's son, Sam, is about to leave for the Liverpool Football Academy, Shelley Hughes's son is being held in a Young Offenders' Institute on a charge of attempted murder. And they are joined by the distant echoes of Wilfred Owen leaving his mother, Susan, to join the Great War effort. As Martha adjusts to life without Sam, her own career begins to haunt her when she becomes embroiled in the sad fate of young Callum Hughes.

With grateful thanks to the Liverpool Football Academy and to Wilfred Owen – without whose genius this would have been a lesser book.

PROLOGUE

Tuesday 6th September, 3.55 p.m.

If only he could reach the gate. He'd tried to slip across the schoolyard, running across the quadrangle, shoulders low, head down, staring at the ground as though this would render him invisible, zigzagging like a pursued hare but one of them had spotted him and alerted the others. Then they had all come streaming towards him, jeering and shouting, dropping their schoolbags to join in the chase. Five of them. While others watched, doing nothing. He put an extra spurt in, tried to outrun them but it was hopeless. His chest was tight and he couldn't breathe. Then he knew he would be beaten. Again. They easily outflanked him. Screaming as they ran like Zulus or Indians or '*the dreaded Hun*'. Three on one side, two on the other, and he knew they would bring him down, kick him on the floor, lay into him. As they'd done before and before that and for as long as he'd been at this damned school.

His chest tightened and he panted, pursued and terrified. Then a soft calm stole over him. He wasn't a victim or a hunted animal but a human being who could fight back. Afterwards he might think that he hadn't wanted it to happen, that he hadn't wanted any of it to happen but he could never be quite sure that that was the truth. Ahead of him, tantalisingly, stood the half open gate. The promise of escape. A glimmer of hope, waiting for him. If he could only reach it, pass through to the other side, to the world outside the school, he would be safe.

Until the next time.

But they were gaining on him. He heard his own breath catching in hoarse, rasping pants, their jeers ringing in his ears, blocking out any other sound now apart from his own heart, pounding.

They were almost upon him.

Just as he reached his hand out, almost touched the gate, someone gripped his shoulder and yanked him back. He tried to shake it off and keep running but he knew it was useless. It was all useless. He was beaten.

Two hands were on him now, one on each shoulder, spinning him round and he stared into the hated face.

'Hey, Wilf. How're you doing?'

They always started like this, with a false friendship only meant to mock.

'All right,' he cast back. 'I'm all right.'

It was the wrong answer. The wrong answer because there was no right answer.

They were all wrong.

But he stopped running now, mumbling instead into the ground. 'Leave me alone, will you?'

Another of them had reached him now, Will Morris, who pushed his fist into his chest. 'And why would we want to do that? You're our sport, Wilf.'

Even the name was meant to mock.

Then, quite suddenly, almost without him being aware of it, the worm turned. His fright melted, sizzling, like ice in a fire. Red mist swirled in front of his eyes and he knew he had finally had enough. He swung his rucksack down from his back, fumbled in it, found the knife. Then, brandishing it in his hand, for once feeling powerful, he turned around and faced them, holding it, like Bernado in *West Side Story*, jabbing.

Without fear.

He gave them fair warning. 'Because it'd be better for you.'

But they still jeered, unimpressed by his fight-back.

'D'you hear that? Wilf's threatening *me*. Well. What about that then? Oh I'm frightened,' DreadNought mocked. 'I am so-o frightened. My heart is going boom bo de boom and my knees are knocking together. I am like jelly.' He did a mock shivery shake and his gang all laughed.

Callum searched the ring of faces, was vaguely aware in the background of open mouths, held breath.

He felt powerful. He could do this. He had practised.

He lunged.

DreadNought moved back. 'Get lost, you psycho.'

His face was filled with derision.

Callum knew then that DreadNought never would take any notice.

So he lunged again.

CHAPTER ONE

5 p.m. the same day

She was always on edge when he was late home from school.

She kept wandering out of the kitchen, into the narrow hallway and back again, wiping her hands on a tea towel, pushing her sleeve up again and again to glance at her watch.

5.05.

She returned to the kitchen to check everything was ready to prepare the meal. Pasta, tuna, tomatoes. Then she scuttled back out into the hallway. She had heard a noise. A car door slamming. So it was that she saw the two dark uniforms, rippled by the glass. And heard their voices, 'I'll handle this, Roberts'.

She froze.

'I won't need those, Mum.'

Martha put the football boots back down on the floor.

'They provide all that,' he said gruffly. Maybe Sam had seen her scrubbing them and felt some tiny measure of guilt.

'So you won't want your...?'

Again he shook his head and she put the sports shirts back in the almost empty drawer.

'I can do it myself, you know,' he said gently. 'They expect you to be independent.'

He stood up, gave her a hug around her waist. 'They encourage it.'

'I *want* to do it. Sam.' She hesitated. There was so much she wanted to say: You'll be all right. Don't be lonely. Keep in touch. Ring, write, text or email, but please keep in touch. Don't become a stranger. Don't grow up too soon – or stay a little boy forever.

But there comes a time when a mother's duty is to let go, not to cling to her son.

Motionless, behind the glass, Shelley Hughes knew that if she even breathed they would pick up on her movement. Even the shallowest breathing is perceptible to the hunter.

She saw a reeded hand rise and knock. Too loud and aggressive to be anything but the police.

So even before she opened the door she already knew that life would never be the same again.

Their faces were hard and hostile. 'Mrs Hughes? Callum Hughes's mother?'

She nodded, not trusting herself to speak.

There were two of them, one gawky and angular, the other fatter, with big thighs and a double chin. He was the one who seemed to be in command.

It was he who spoke, flashing an ID card at her. 'We're police officers. Can we come in?'

She stood back and they filed past her into the small, tidy sitting room.

Where is Callum? Where is Callum? Where is my son? The

refrain repeated through her mind, over and over again, blanking everything else out.

'What is it?' Fear iced her voice with aggression.

Both the officers were standing, awkwardly, in the centre of the room, eyes flicking away from her face.

'I'm afraid we've got some bad news.'

For a moment she believed her son was dead.

She sank down on the sofa, feeling the room slip away from her, only vaguely aware of the gawky copper bending over her.

'He's been involved in an incident. I'm sorry?'

Her mind floated away to wonder, Why should *he* be sorry? He didn't *know* Callum. Then she drifted back down to ask fuzzily, '*Incident? Incident? What sort of incident? Is he hurt?*'

The gawky copper took pity on her. 'No, Mrs Hughes. He's not hurt.'

Then, what have they done to him?

She looked from one to the other, eventually finding the words to say coldly, 'What *sort* of incident?'

The two detectives exchanged glances. She knew that neither of them wanted to tell her.

Again the burly one took command. 'It appears, Mrs Hughes,' he said carefully, 'that he's committed a serious assault.'

The rough in her surfaced then. '*Who says?*'

The gawky one took over, some sympathy gleaming in his dark eyes. 'There are plenty of witnesses.'

She retrieved a little dignity, straightened up. 'To what exactly?'

'He knifed someone.'

'In self-defence?'

'No one saw the other boy do anything.'

No one ever did. It was part of the cleverness, almost as though they had been working up to this very moment.

'Is Callum hurt?'

Two – slow – shakes of the head, the action done with regret.

'And the boy – the one he is – *alleged* to have assaulted?'

'He's in hospital with a punctured lung.'

'Is he likely to die?'

'We don't think so.'

'Can I see my son?'

The burly one nodded, shifted his weight to the other foot. His trousers were tight around the fat thighs. He looked uncomfortable. 'We'll take you to him now, if you like. But it'd be a good idea if you packed a few clothes first, Mrs Hughes.' His eyes slid away from hers. 'He's likely to remain in custody for a bit.'

She went upstairs.

What should she pack?

Clothes, toothpaste, his Game Boy, shower gel and shampoo. Pyjamas? What would he be allowed? Chocolate? A monster bag of his favourite crisps? She didn't know.

Martha was surreptitiously studying her son. Sam, like Martin, was not hefty or tall, but lithe, slim and wiry which was why he had been picked. He was fast and cunning on his feet, able to swerve and dodge without losing his balance, at the same time watching where the other players were on the field. She had watched him and recognised this talent. And so had the scouts from the Liverpool Football Academy.

She recalled the day they had spoken to her.

'The boys love it there. They're happy. It becomes their family. *Better* than a family. The other players are their brothers, the coaches like fathers.'

'And their mothers?'

The question had made the men uncomfortable. Had she strained she might have eavesdropped on their thoughts. As it was she saw the sentiment flash between them.

How much does a growing lad need a mother?

But instead of addressing the issue they ploughed on with their spiel. 'It's a great chance for your son, Mrs Gunn. Most lads would jump at the chance to go to Anfield. It's a privilege. Be pleased for him, Mrs Gunn.'

She was – but...

'It's the beginning of a career.'

And she had wondered. The *right* career? Football? And felt forced to ask.

'And if he doesn't make the grade?'

'If he doesn't make Liverpool there'll be plenty of other clubs where he can apply. We look after our prodigies, Mrs Gunn. They all do well. We wouldn't have picked him otherwise.'

What does a mother say to her son at a time like this?

Be careful?

Be patriotic?

Make me proud of you?

Stay out of danger?

Stay alive?

And the son?

What does he say?
Confess his apprehension or...
Jauntily...
'I am the British Army.'

Shelley looked out of the windows of the police car. It was a dazzling September afternoon. The traffic looked hot. The roads looked hot. The people looked hot. The weather always did this, cheered up as soon as the children returned to school. It had been typically cool and wet right through August. She caught the eye of one or two of the curious neighbours and bent her head, ashamed.

They drove her to the police station in Monkmoor and dropped her outside on the steps. The police inside were more polite than the general public. No one caught her eyes or showed undue interest. The two officers joined her and took her straight to an interview room.

All the way there she had been steeling herself for the sight of her son in police custody. But as she entered the room she was struck by how familiar Callum looked. It was only as she drew nearer that she picked up on the detail. As they say: The devil is in the detail. Through the thin shirt of his school uniform he was quivering with fear. His face was white, his eyes scared. 'Callum,' she said.

'Mum. I'm sorry.'

She took in more detail. Her son was sitting at a shabby table in a shabby room. His school blazer was hung over the back of the chair, his schoolbag – a Quiksilver rucksack – dumped on the floor beside him.

She wanted to put her arms around him, hug him, stroke

the gelled hair and reassure him that everything would be all right. But she knew it wouldn't.

'I'm sorry, Mum,' he said again. Later she would take some consolation from the fact that his eyes did not shrink from hers, that instead, they held honesty. That and relief that she was here.

'Hello, Call.' She spoke steadily, inviting his trust, the old myth, *Dulce at Decorum Est*. She put the suitcase in the corner, hoping he hadn't noticed and if he had that he would not read the grim message that it signified.

There was nothing sweet or honourable about this.

She sat down opposite her son and managed a watery smile. 'You'd better tell me what happened.'

The bulky police officer cleared his throat with a harsh rasp. 'Best we wait for the duty solicitor, Mrs Hughes. He won't be long.'

She swivelled her head so he would know that she understood what he was doing.

And so the four of them faced each other across the table and waited silently.

'You're not worried about this, Sam, are you?'

Martha had half turned and caught a look of fleeting apprehension on her son's face.

''Course not,' he said scornfully. 'I can't wait to go, Mum. You know that.'

It was the last three words, heavy with bravado, that told her all.

'Good,' she said steadily. 'And being away from home?'

He rolled his eyes ceilingwards. 'I'll be glad to get away

from this Abba den. Any more of this and I'll go mental. Honestly, Mum, I'll love it.'

'Initially,' she said cautiously, 'it'll only be for a year. You understand that. At the end of the year they'll be able to decide one way or the other.'

Again Sam shrugged. 'If I'm good enough I'll be in. If not it's better I get on with other things. OK?'

She nodded and carried on folding the sea of clothes. Vests, T-shirts, socks, pants, jackets, shirts, ties. Young Liverpool must never appear scruffily dressed but little gentlemen. *Self-confidence and opportunity*. She recalled the blurb in the numerous brochures she had been sent as the prospective parent.

She smiled. And wasn't it odd that the one group of items missing was sports strip. It would all be provided by The Club. Another buzz phrase.

Finally, she managed to lock the suitcase and waited patiently downstairs, knowing that Sam would need some time to say goodbye to his twin sister. Martha sat on the bottom step, smiling. The twin sister, who appeared an entire pole apart from her brother. She, blonde, he darker; she, a party girl, he, a team player. He, wiry and strong, she, slim as a reed. And yet they were two albeit dissimilar peas from the very same pod.

She could hear them upstairs. 'Promise you'll text me – every day.' Sukey's high pitched order.

Sam's gruff reply. 'I might not have time, Sukes.'

'You'd better. And Mum's said we'll come up and see some of your matches.'

'No screaming then.'

'Not even if you're about to score the most wonderful goal?'

'Most of all not then,' Sam warned. 'You'll distract me.'

Martha was startled. When had Sam's voice turned quite so gruff? When had he begun to sound like an adult male?

She wasn't sure. Children do this. You watch them like a hawk, sure you will be the first to spot any change. And then, just at the point when you are distracted, they morph, straight into the next stage of their development. You turn your head and the chrysalis is shedding its wrapping; turn your head again and the wings are unfolding. She felt a strange, painful pull on her heart.

The silence gave Shelley an opportunity to watch Callum and muse. Why? Even looking at him through a mother's eyes she could see that Callum looked a loser. Thin and small for his age, a late-developer. Not smart or sporty but an asthma sufferer who had frequently had time off school. Her mouth twisted. Someone born to be picked on.

If he'd had a dad. It was a familiar thought which she swiftly rejected. He was better off without him.

The solicitor turned up forty minutes later. Scruffily suited, a bulging briefcase under his arm which he put on the floor. He took out a large notepad and placed it in front of him, on the desk.

Then he grinned at Callum. 'Hello,' he said, extending a large hand. 'I'm Wesley Stephenson. I'm the duty solicitor and for now I'm in charge of your case.'

Callum shook the proffered hand with apathy.

He's losing hope, Shelley thought. Already he's giving up.

'I'm Callum's mother, Shelley,' she said. She would not go down the path of despair.

The solicitor turned to the police. 'I'll have a quiet word with my client, if that's OK. Is that all right with you, Callum?'

''Spose so.'

Callum looked down at the floor.

For a brief moment no one spoke.

In the end it was Shelley who broke the silence.

'DreadNought was bullying him,' she said roughly. 'He'd been picking on my lad for nearly a year now. Callum was only defending himself.' She plucked a phrase from the newspapers. 'I thought that was justifiable.'

'Reasonable force,' the solicitor said calmly, his eyes moving from Callum to his mother. 'I understand that Roger Gough was not carrying a weapon.'

'There was *more* of them,' Callum said truculently. 'How else was I going to make them see I meant business?' He tried a joke. 'I'm not exactly built like Arnold Schwarzenegger, am I?'

The solicitor took the top off his fountain pen, drew the notepad nearer to him. 'Why don't you start at the beginning?'

'All right. It was a couple of years ago,' Callum said. And dulling his tone was the conviction that no one would believe him. 'My asthma was bad and DreadNought started picking on me. Him and his gang. Will Morris, Gareth Sigley and the rest.'

The solicitor started writing, looked up. 'I shall need *all* their names.'

Callum nodded grumpily.

'What did they do?'

'Mainly took my schoolbag so I never had the right books or schoolwork and got into trouble. Then they started chucking things at me, tearing my clothes, asking for money like they do some of the others. But I never seemed to have enough money so they got more nasty.'

'Go on.'

'They pushed me in the river once, off the Porthill footbridge.'

'My lad doesn't swim,' Shelley said, pressing her lips together. 'He might have drowned.'

'Did no one see this?'

Callum gave him a look of pity. 'Yeah,' he said. 'Plenty of people *saw* it. But they didn't see what was happening. What they saw was a load of rowdy lads fooling about.'

'So?'

'So – someone fished me out and never stopped rollicking me for being stupid and drunk. I wasn't either, Mr Stephenson.'

Wesley Stephenson gave Callum a reassuring smile and an encouraging nod.

'Then they'd start threatening me. Telling lies, saying I'd flashed at one of the girls in the class. She's DreadNought's girlfriend and she knows as well as me that I did nothing of the sort. She just made it up to fall in with her boyfriend.'

'The girl's name, Callum?'

'Katie Ashbourne. She lives a couple of doors away from me.' Callum flushed right up to the roots of his mousy hair.

'Is she a good-looking girl?'

Callum looked down at the table, nodded miserably.

And Shelley could see it all. Callum had fancied the very girl who had furthered the myth. The love of his enemy.

And looking at Wesley Stephenson she could see that he had understood this too. There was a moment of empathy between them as they exchanged glances.

'So this went on for a year or two?'

Callum nodded.

'And then?'

'Over the weekend I was walking in the Quarry and I saw them walking towards me. I started to run away and they just laughed. I knew then that they'd won. They'd made me into a coward – someone who runs away so...'

'You went into town and bought a knife.'

Another miserable nod.

'On the corner of Roushill there's one of those shops that sells everything. You know – it's old-fashioned. It's got coal-scuttles and doormats and things hanging up outside. I just went in and said my mum had asked me to get a carving knife for the Sunday joint. The old lady got all sorts out and I chose one.' He looked furtively into the corner of the room, head dipped, shoulders up defensively.

The solicitor had noticed the action too. 'And?'

'I bought a sharpening stone, too.'

Shelley's heart smashed to the floor. This was the worst part. She was intelligent enough to translate the action into legal terms. Not only intent but *malicious* intent. She looked helplessly at Stephenson. They would get him for this.

Stephenson was staring abstractedly at the wall. She could almost hear him cursing.

'And then?'

'I put it in my schoolbag ready for when they came at me again.' Callum paused. 'And they did – today – after school. They started like they always did, shouting after me, calling me names. So I got my knife out and threatened him with it. DreadNought just laughed.' He paused to think. 'It was that really. Even with a big sharp knife in my hand they didn't take me seriously so I went for him. I stuck it in.' He looked pleadingly at his mother then at the solicitor. 'It went in easily,' he said. 'Like a knife into soft butter.' He smiled. 'I read that once, that the knife actually slips in quite easily and I didn't quite believe it. In fact I can remember I was thinking, *I can't believe it's not butter*. I was laughing. Then DreadNought started gasping. I saw the blood. People were screaming and looking at me as though I had gone completely off my rocker. I think someone grabbed the knife off me. Someone else got hold of me and wrestled me to the ground. The police came – and an ambulance. I'm sorry. I don't remember much more.'

The solicitor took off his glasses and stared at them. Then he put them back on his nose. 'You don't have to tell me this, Callum,' he said, 'but what was in your mind? What did you intend to do with the knife?'

'I don't know. Make them afraid of me like I'd been afraid of them. Prove to myself and to them that I wasn't a coward.'

The solicitor sighed. 'You must have had *some* idea what you were going to do with it. Let me help you. I'll give you some ideas. Did you think you'd wave it at them and frighten them so they'd stop?'

Callum stared at the floor. 'Not really.'

'Did you think, I just want him to stop?'

Callum eyed the solicitor. He knew full well what Stephenson was asking.

'Or did you intend to kill him? The defence,' he continued smoothly, 'will make much of the fact that you sharpened an already-sharp knife. Also that the injury was near the heart. You could be on a murder charge. As it is you could well be on a charge of attempted murder. We might get it reduced to grievous bodily harm but the charges are serious.'

Shelley's mouth was dry. They would take her boy away from her. He would be sent down. No community service charge this one. He would be incarcerated in a place which was full of DreadNoughts and their gangs.

'I don't know if I meant to kill him,' Callum said. 'I think even at the time I didn't know.' He looked away from them both, weighing up the choices, almost fascinated by the different interpretations of the same act.

'Right.' Stephenson wrote rapidly in his notebook. 'Let's get the police in. If there's anything you don't want to answer just say 'No comment.' Don't volunteer information. Let me do most of the talking.'

Callum nodded, his lips pressed together.

He'd got the message.

Stephenson called the two policemen in. He made a good case, explained about the continuing assaults.

While the two policemen watched, their eyes hard and narrow and disbelieving, they didn't even try to hide their scepticism.

And they asked the questions that she dreaded in the ponderous, pedantic language of the law.

'Was anyone a witness to these *alleged* attacks by the injured boy?'

'Plenty of people.'

The policeman sat, pen poised.

'No one what'd say.'

The policeman sighed. 'Just give us some names.'

Callum pressed his lips together even harder. 'You don't get it, do you? They're frightened he'd turn on them. They won't say a word to you.'

The lawyer pushed his pad towards the youth. 'Just write the names.'

In a slow, ponderous hand, Callum Hughes wrote:

Katie Ashbourne, Chelsea Arnold, Charmaine Nash, Will Morris, Gareth Sigley. He thought for a minute then continued, *Roberto Pantini* and *Dave Arrett.* Then he looked up.

'You're wasting your time,' he said. 'They're all in the gang. You won't get one of them to say anything good about me.'

The lawyer persisted. 'Who's your best friend?'

It drew the evasive look again. 'Haven't really got one,' Callum muttered. 'Once you're out of it you're too dangerous to make a friend of.'

'Do you get on well with any of your teachers?'

Callum shrugged.

'Well what's your favourite subject?'

'History.' At last there was a spark of life in the boy. ''Specially World War One.'

'Any particular aspect?' The solicitor asked more out of curiosity.

'All of it.' A tentative, hesitant smile. 'That's why I gave DreadNought his name.'

'I see.'

Martha shouted up the stairs. 'Time to go, Sam.'

'OK. Bye, Sis.' The valediction was accompanied by thunderous footsteps down the stairs which suddenly smote a pang at Martha's heart. Oh, but she would miss him. The noise, the dirty football strip, the ever-playing football reruns, the cocky boyish comments. 'He could have got that one.'

From now on they would be an exclusively female household.

And how would Sam fit in with the others at the academy?

She couldn't resist it. She rumpled his hair as he passed, provoking an objection, 'Mu-u-m.'

Bobby, tail wagging, was licking Sam's hand. He gave a little woof of approval and Sam bent and kissed the thick, black fur. 'Goodbye, old chum,' he said hoarsely. 'I'm going to miss yer. Be good. Don't catch too many rabbits.'

Bobby gave another soft, sad bark.

Together they loaded the two suitcases into the back of the car and Sam strapped himself into the passenger seat. Martha slammed the door behind him, got into her side, started the engine and accelerated down the drive, Sam giving his home one last, long look, waving frantically as he spotted Sukey and Agnetha in an upstairs window.

Bobby chased them enthusiastically down the drive for a hundred yards or so before giving up and merely sitting forlornly in the middle of the lane, his brown eyes following them until they disappeared round the corner, when he stood up and trotted back to his sentry post, outside the front door.

Sam gave a deep sigh and settled back in his seat. Martha sneaked a look across at him. He was frowning hard, trying not to be a baby, hoping she would not notice. 'Bit of music?' she asked and switched on the car radio – low – in case he wanted to talk.

CHAPTER TWO

8 p.m.

The police didn't believe a word of it. Or if they did it didn't make any difference to Callum's assault. Shelley could see that. She watched both their faces very carefully, saw them exchange glances, smirking as the solicitor explained that Callum had been provoked, that this had not been an attack out of the blue.

She felt like saying out loud, challenging the coppers, making them understand that her son was not a psychopath, that he was simply a youth who had been pushed too far.

They saw Roger Gough as innocent, her son as the guilty one. It riled her.

'With respect,' the burly one, whose name, she learned through the taped introductions, was Sergeant Paul Talith, 'can anyone verify this tale? I mean...' He leaned far back in his chair, meaty thighs wide apart, double chin bulging. 'We've been taking statements and no one's said anything about Roger Gough. They all say...'

His cynicism fired Callum into action. 'What a nice boy he is?' he sneered. 'What a little saint he is?' He glared at Paul Talith. 'It's bullshit. Believe all that crap and you'd believe

Jack the Ripper was a Sunday school teacher. He was beating the shit out of me a couple of times a week.'

The policeman leaned forward and locked eyes. 'Prove it,' he said.

And Shelley watched her son wither.

Martha was driving north out of Shrewsbury, along the A49, towards Whitchurch. It should have been a fast road but there seemed always to be a slower car in front of them holding them up so Martha barely touched 45mph. When a tractor pulled out right in front of them Sam became impatient. 'They said to try and get there before nine,' he said. 'I don't want to be late. It wouldn't *look* good.'

'We've got ages.' Martha's eyes left the road for a split second to look at him. How young he seemed. With more than a little essence of Martin. She steadied herself and gripped the steering wheel. 'When do you come home next?'

'There's a couple of days off next month.' Sam spoke nonchalantly, kicking the floor with his trainers.

Martha rose to the bait. 'Oh, that's good. I can come and get you. It's not far anyway.'

'It'll just be for a weekend,' Sam warned. 'I expect I'll have to come back on the Sunday night.'

'You can have a late lunch with us, maybe a bit of a walk with Bobby. You know.'

'Mum,' he said, suddenly urgent, 'what if I don't like it? What if I absolutely hate it? What if the other guys are beasts? What if I want to come home?'

'Then we shall have to discuss it,' Martha said, eyes now fixed firmly on the road. 'But you have to give it a chance. I have an idea,' she said, as she paused at the roundabout, ready to take the A49 north. 'What about if we have a secret code?'

'What do you mean?' Sam sounded far from convinced.

'Well,' she said, warming to her subject. 'I read somewhere that Wilfred Owen, the poet,' she glanced across maybe Sam wouldn't appreciate the analogy, 'you know that he went away to war – the First World War?'

'Ye-es?'

'He wasn't allowed to tell anyone where he was or where he was going'

Sam was watching her.

'In case his letter fell into enemy hands.'

'You mean the Germans?'

'Yes. So he and his mother devised a Mistletoe code. If he used the word mistletoe the letters of the next few lines spelt out where he was going, like *Serre*, in France. So how about if you text me to say that you hope Bobby is fine *I* know that you're OK. If, on the other hand, you say that you hope he isn't catching too many mice then I know there's a problem and I should either give you a ring or pop up sooner rather than later.'

'Ace,' Sam said, with satisfaction, sinking back into the seat, a wide grin across his face. 'It can be our own, special private mistletoe code so we can communicate and no one will know what we're really saying.'

Isn't it strange how most young males love their spot of intrigue?

She looked at him, suddenly swamped with a wave of affection.

Courage was mine, and I had mystery
Wisdom was mine, and I had mastery.

* * *

'Tell me about the knife.'

It was the younger, skinny policeman who asked this. PC Gethin Roberts, according to the taped introductions. 'Where did you buy it from?'

'At Birch's – the shop on the corner of Roushill and Smithfield Road.'

To the right of Callum, Stephenson started rubbing his neck. He always did this when he didn't like the answer his client was returning. And Hughes's answer couldn't have been worse. He knew the shop. It was not a busy, bustling supermarket store where Callum Hughes might have slipped in, made his purchases and slipped out again without anyone remembering, but a family-run business which prided itself on personal service. The name was painted in huge, black letters on a whitewashed wall, C.R.Birch&Son. They would remember the boy and they would also remember that at the same time as he had bought the knife, he had purchased a sharpening stone. So that little bit of evidence was bound to come out – and be made much of by the prosecution.

Stephenson heaved a big, private sigh. He always got landed with them, he reflected, these naive ones. The quiet ones. The weirdoes, the still waters who ran so deep and lashed out without warning. His gaze landed back on the boy and he wondered what was going on inside that strange head of his?

Maybe Callum picked up on the solicitor's sigh. He turned his head and stared at him. For a split second they exchanged something – some empathy. Stephenson cleared his throat and for some unaccountable reason was reminded of his two-year-old son, Dylan, who sometimes stared at him with the same perceptive and unabashed absorption.

He took his glasses off and wiped them on a tissue he drew from his pocket. It wouldn't do to feel pity for this soul or to connect him too closely to his own child. And yet... He turned his attention towards Shelley. Callum was her son just as Dylan was his and Andrea's.

Both the police were watching him impatiently. He read their minds.

Get on with it.

'You were seen...' PC Gethin Roberts was reading from some notes he'd made earlier '...by many witnesses getting the knife from your bag and approaching Roger Gough with it in your hand. Do you deny that you took the knife with the intention of assaulting your schoolmate?'

Callum shook his head. Even he could work out that it would be pointless. Everyone had seen it in his hand, for goodness' sake. He supposed he could have said he'd *found* it, in his schoolbag, by chance. But that was so weak. And for once in his life he didn't want to be weak.

'For the record defendant has shaken his head.' PC Roberts spoke.

'Why did you have a knife?' Paul Talith's style of questioning was very different. Truculent and confrontational.

'I don't know.'

'I suggest to you that you know perfectly well why you had a knife. It was to attack Roger Gough, wasn't it?'

Callum opened his mouth to deny it then thought, what the Hell? 'Yes,' he said instead.

'I suppose you disliked the guy.' Talith couldn't manage to be subtle – even when he tried as hard as this.

'I did dislike him. Why don't you ask me why?'

Talith simply lifted his eyebrows.

'It was because he was bullying me.'

'Look, sonny.' Again Talith leaned right across the table. 'We don't have any evidence that Gough was anything but a school buddy of yours. You, on the other hand, were seen plunging a knife right into Roger Gough's chest missing his heart by a couple of inches. It was a lethal attack. Understand? He's lucky to be alive. In fact,' he jabbed his finger at Callum, '*you're* damned lucky he's still alive. You don't know how lucky you are, sonny. You could well have been up on a murder charge.'

Callum put his hand to his throat and drew in a long, rasping breath.

'Pass his inhaler,' Shelley ordered. 'Give it to him.'

Roberts handed the schoolbag across to her. Disdain darkening her face, she fished out a Ventolin pump and handed it to Callum without saying a word. They all watched silently while he inhaled two sharp squirts.

Roberts waited for a minute or two then continued with the questioning. 'Tell me about the knife,' he said. 'When did you buy it?'

'I told you. A week ago.'

'*Why* did you buy it?'

'I don't know. Self defence I suppose.'

'So you did intend to use it against someone.'

'I don't know.'

'Was it for anyone specific?'

'I don't know.'

'Have you ever stabbed anyone before?'

Callum shook his emphatically. 'No, I never have.'

'So you bought it with a *specific* purpose in mind.' The way he lingered over the word specific was a lure, a shining thing in the water, dangling for him to take it in his mouth. But then he would be caught – trapped and never free without tearing his flesh.

Callum appealed dumbly to Stephenson.

'My client has no comment.'

'Did you intend to *kill* him?'

The question brought the wild look into the lad's eyes. For one brief second everyone in the small interview room held their breath.

The solicitor was the first to regain his equilibrium. 'My client has no comment,' he said but he knew the damage had been done. They had all seen and interpreted the expression in Callum Hughes's eyes. These were the same mad eyes which had stared out of his face as he had driven the knife into Roger Gough's lung. And if his arm had not been restrained by a teacher who knows what might have happened next?

There was a knock on the door and a tall, slim detective entered.

Gethin Roberts spoke into the tape recorder. 'Detective Inspector Randall has entered the room at 19.46. Interrogation suspended.'

The two policemen shut off the machine and muttered to the detective in the corner. Once or twice Alex Randall glanced across at Callum, his intelligent eyes appraising the situation, resting on the lad with interest.

Paul Talith muttered something under his breath and Alex Randall looked again – at Shelley Hughes this time. She pretended not to notice his scrutiny but when Randall had turned his gaze back to his colleagues she stole another glance at him.

'Tasty,' she thought, before scolding herself. What was she thinking of – fancying a copper – and the one that had her son in custody at that.

'You'd better charge him,' Alex Randall was saying. 'We'll keep him here overnight and get him in front of the magistrates in the morning. Get some paperwork together.'

Paul Talith said something and they all heard Randall's reply. 'Attempted murder. If that doesn't stick we've got plenty of other charges. Come on, Talith. You know the score.'

Randall approached Callum then, stopping right in front of the interview desk, his long figure leaning in towards the boy. 'Listen, son,' he said, 'take my advice. Don't make this any more difficult for yourself than it has to be. You've got a tough enough time ahead without making enemies of the coppers who will treat you well and make sure you get a fair trial.'

Callum lifted his eyes without hope. He shrugged and said nothing. Randall put his hand on the door then turned to speak to Roberts. 'Have you rung the hospital?'

Roberts shook his head.

'Well – I suggest you do.'

When Alex Randall had left the room Paul Talith stood up. 'I'll get you some drinks,' he said to Shelley, Callum and Stephenson. 'Give you a chance to have a bit of a chat.' He jerked his head towards the door and the two officers filed out.

As soon as the door had closed behind them Shelley spoke

to Callum. 'Tell that Inspector Randall the truth,' she said. 'He looks a decent sort, as though he'd believe you. Tell *him* about DreadNought and the others. He'll understand. I know he will.' She appealed to the solicitor then. 'If they can say Call was *pushed* into it surely it'll make a difference?'

The solicitor cleared his throat. 'Some,' he said. 'Not quite as much as you might think. But we can explain about the provocation later on when the case comes to the Crown Court. It doesn't alter the facts of the crime, Mrs Hughes.'

She looked fiercely at him. 'But it makes *all* the difference. If that little rat hadn't picked on my son none of this would have happened. If the school had stopped DreadNought in his tracks he wouldn't be in hospital today. And Callum wouldn't be here,' she finished viciously.

The solicitor tried to pacify her. 'True – true but we'll have time enough to gather some information on that later.'

Shelley pressed her lips together and satisfied herself with a rebellious stare.

Callum touched his mother's hand. 'That detective won't be able to do anything for me, Mum. I don't know why you trust him. You know what these coppers are like. They've got their case. That's all they care about. Nothing to do with *justice*. They're not going to try and paint me any whiter than I am.' He dropped his head onto his folded arms.

Her eyes landed on the closed door. 'They're not all like that. Some of them must be decent. *He* seems decent.'

'He's still a copper.'

'Ahem, ahem.' Wesley Stephenson cleared his throat. 'We don't have a lot of time. We shouldn't waste it, Callum. Let's recap. You were seen by countless witnesses to pull a knife from your schoolbag and deliberately stick it in Roger Gough's chest. I take it that's true?'

Callum nodded.

'And the knife you'd used you'd bought the week before together with a sharpener from the same shop. That too is true, I take it.'

Again Callum nodded miserably.

'And you actually *used* the sharpening stone...?'

Another nod.

'Are there any witnesses to your bullying who would confirm your story?'

This time a slow, regretful shake of the head. 'There's witnesses all right,' Callum said. 'But none of them'll speak out. They're too afraid of DreadNought.'

'OK.' The solicitor tried again. 'Apart from your school chums might anybody know something?' He looked at Shelley. 'Did either of you discuss this bullying with anyone – priest, doctor, teacher – anyone?'

Both Shelley and Callum hung their heads.

'And you never sought medical help following any of the attacks?'

Another slow shake of the head.

All three people present could see how dark the case was.

The solicitor was quiet for a moment. 'And you say that...'

Then Shelley looked up. 'I did ring the doctor once,' she said, 'to ask him what to do about broken ribs.'

'Think carefully about this, Shelley,' Stephenson said, hardly daring to hope. 'Did you mention Callum?'

'No. I just asked what you should do if *someone* had broken ribs,' she said. 'I didn't say Call.'

'Which doctor?'

'Doctor Porter at the Health Centre,' she said, still with the same heart-breaking hopefulness in her voice.

The brief made a note to himself to speak to the doctor. 'Can you remember when it was?'

'Six months ago. April, May time.'

'Good.' He addressed his next question to Callum. 'Did it seem probable that you *had* broken a rib?'

Callum shrugged. 'Don't know. They had me on the floor and were kicking me. I had a bad pain in my right side for a couple of months after that but I don't know.'

The solicitor made a mental note to suggest they have some x-rays done.

'Now then, Callum, did DreadNought ever bully anyone else?'

Callum frowned as he concentrated.

'Anyone at all,' the brief prompted.

'A girl, Chelsea. She used to be friends with Katie but they fell out.' He flushed. 'DreadNought pushed her really hard once down some steps in school. She broke her wrist. She was in plaster for ages after.'

'Her full name?'

'Chelsea Arnold. She lives up in Harlescott near Morrisons. Her dad works on the buses.'

'She goes to your school?'

Callum nodded.

'Then I'll find her,' Wesley Stephenson promised.

He put a hand on Callum's shoulder. 'Callum,' he said, 'is there anyone who could speak up for you? Say that you were of good character, vouch for you as a decent person?'

Again hope briefly flared and died in the boy's face. 'Mr Farthing,' he said. 'My history teacher. But...he was the one who stopped me sticking the knife into DreadNought again. He caught my hand and took the knife off me. He knew I would have killed him.'

Stephenson's heart sank. From worse to terrible. That described this case. Each time he thought he had heard the worst scenario something else cropped up which made the situation deteriorate further. 'Callum,' he said again. 'Listen to me carefully now. We can't deny facts. My job isn't to *get you off*. Do you realise that? If I was the most brilliant lawyer in the land I couldn't do that. Not with all those witnesses who saw what happened. We can't even say that the knife was in your bag by accident or that you were carrying a knife for some other purpose such as woodwork or a hobby. Our defence will rest on a few points. One – that this assault was out of character – in other words that you are, by nature, a peaceable and quiet individual. Two, that you were provoked into attacking Roger Gough, that it was done in self-defence and also that while you meant to scare him off, you did not mean to kill him. Do you understand all that I've said?'

Callum nodded.

'Have there been any other incidents which might be brought up in court?'

Callum shook his head.

Stephenson doubted it. In these sorts of cases there was always something else. What he didn't want was for him to hear it for the first time in the court. He would be in combat without a shield.

'Right,' he said, then turned back to Shelley. 'What about Callum's dad? Might we call on him?'

'You won't get anything from him,' Shelley Hughes said bitterly. 'We haven't heard from him for years.'

'Does he give any financial support?'

Shelley withered him with a look.

'I see.'

There was a knock on the door and Sergeant Paul Talith and PC Roberts filed back in. They spoke woodenly to Wesley Stephenson. 'We're going to caution and charge your client.'

Stephenson nodded, accepting the inevitable but Callum stared from one to the other, his face as white as chalk. 'I'll go to prison then, won't I, Mr Stephenson,' he whispered.

Shelley drew in a sharp breath.

'You'll be in front of the magistrate tomorrow,' the solicitor answered. 'I doubt that she'll grant bail in such a serious case. You'll almost certainly be in remand until your case can be heard in a Crown Court.'

'How long will that take,' Shelley demanded, her face as taut as wire.

'They'll be as quick as possible in view of your son's age.' Stephenson was hedging.

'How long?'

'A few months.'

'And then?'

'I think you should be prepared for a custodial sentence.'

'Prison?' Callum's voice was a squeak.

'You're too young to go to prison, Callum. You'll go to a Young Offenders' Institution.'

'And it'll be full of people like DreadNought.'

'There will be some like that,' the Brief said. But most of them, he added mentally, will be youngsters like you. Weak, unhappy, sad, vulnerable.

Callum's eyes refused to leave him. 'Then I might as well be dead.'

They had arrived at Knowsley, a few miles east of Liverpool between the A580 and the M57. Martha consulted her map and soon picked up the signs and as she saw the first one she felt a sudden surge of pride. *Her* son. *Her* lad, the boy she had brought up single-handedly, had aimed so high, achieved so much.

To be here was like a Christian standing outside the gates of Heaven. She moved the car forward and was immediately challenged by a ponderous guard. She had to present ID and the letter of introduction. There was heavy security around the perimeter. An electric fence and electric eyes which swivelled and watched her as she drove up the drive.

They found their way to the reception and were met by a business-like woman in her early forties who carried a clipboard. She smiled at Sam. 'Ah, yes,' she said. 'Sam Gunn. I've been looking forward to meeting you. Welcome to Liverpool. We hope you'll be happy here. Here's to your first goal then, son.'

For some silly reason Martha Gunn, sensible coroner but proud mother, bristled at this woman calling Sam her son. Wasn't it enough that they were taking him away? With strict rules about home visits and contact? Did they also want to deprive her of any role in his very existence?

The woman gave her a searching look. 'My name's Christine Sweetman, Mrs Gunn.' She gave a warm smile. 'I expect you'll be missing him.'

Martha tried to toss it off with a headshake – and knew she had failed.

'Yes,' she finally acknowledged simply. It was the honest answer. Through the window she could see boys playing football in their red strip. Sam's eyes drifted across and she knew he was almost oblivious to her presence, he was already absorbed in watching the play, noting each player's moves, speed, deftness. Footballers do this, store to a giant memory as huge as a cinema screen, every twist, every turn, every movement of a player. She looked too but without the absorption or perception that Sam had. You can only really understand a game if you have played it yourself and apart from knockarounds in the garden she had not ever played a game of football. All *she* really took in was that they were wearing Liverpool strip and looked about Sam's age and that they seemed to have control of the ball as though it was connected to their feet by an invisible length of elastic.

She looked back at her son and knew, like countless mothers before and after her, that he had moved on, away from her influence. Her time was coming to an end. Other people now would assume importance. At thirteen years old he was moving towards different horizons.

'You'll want to meet the principal.'

He turned out to be a smart man in his fifties, an ex-footballer himself, still trim and fit with well-cut greying hair and a strong Liverpool accent.

'Don't you worry about a thing, Mrs Gunn,' he said, putting a friendly arm around her shoulders. 'We'll take good care of your son. I'll look after him as though he were my own. Better in fact.' He laughed loudly at his own joke and she joined in.

He was friendly and fun and she could trust Sam's welfare to him. He would be a father-figure. A substitute for Martin. She smiled.

'Now that's better,' he said. 'I suggest you go and say goodbye to the lad and then head off back home.'

Sam was patently worried that she would kiss him or 'blub'. He scowled at her nervously and backed away. Which hurt her. However, to her credit she committed neither of his fears but ruffled his hair, gave the cheeriest of smiles and said goodbye quickly. She shook hands with the principal and Ms Sweetman and walked back to her car equally quickly. It wasn't until she had driven halfway on the lone return journey that she allowed herself the luxury of a few tears. For company she switched on the radio and picked up the tail end of a track on a golden oldies pop station and listened to some hits of the 70s.

'Callum Hughes, you are charged that on the sixth of September 2005 you did attempt to murder Roger Gough at Hallow's Lane Comprehensive School. You do not have to say anything, but it may harm your defence...'

Callum watched the police, his face white and frightened. And all Shelley could think of was that she was going to have to leave him here.

Like Martha she too drove home alone.

CHAPTER THREE

Wednesday 7th September, 8 a.m.

Callum Hughes was to appear in front of the magistrates at nine o'clock. They woke him at seven to give him time to wash and have his breakfast but they needn't have bothered. He was already awake when they opened his cell door. Lying on his back, staring up at the ceiling, wondering how on earth he could carry on living.

And he didn't want any breakfast anyway.

Shelley hadn't slept a wink all night either. It had been the hardest thing she had ever done, leaving Callum in the police station and returning to an empty house, which, paradoxically, seemed fuller of his presence than when he was at home. She had sat on her sofa, the television turned off and the curtains drawn, and relived again and again the worst moments, answering the door, listening without understanding to the police's bald statements, packing the suitcase, sending him the silent message that he would stay here while she was free to go home. She had looked full into his face and seen his lip curl in a sort of *'et tu Brute'* expression. She had tried to explain that she was not abandoning him or doubting his integrity, merely accepting what she was powerless to change. She had clung to the belief that he had understood this even as Sergeant Talith had lifted the case from her. 'I'll see he gets what he needs,' he'd said and she knew he would check its contents before letting her son have it.

She felt even more weary as the radio alarm clicked on at six-thirty – far too early. But she showered anyway, had two cups of coffee and an orange juice, put on her smartest black skirt, knee-high boots, a white long-sleeved T-shirt and pressed Callum's one and only smart jacket – apart from his blazer which was now bagged up and heading for forensics. She consoled herself with cups of tea until at eight-fifteen she drove to the courthouse. Wesley Stephenson greeted her on the steps. One of her newfound friends. Silently she handed him the bag of clothes.

It was hard not to cry out as Callum was brought to the bench, flanked by the same two police officers as yesterday, Talith and Roberts – two more names which would become more familiar. Shelley looked at her son anxiously. His face was white, his eyes sunken into his face and she knew that he had not slept through the long hours of the night either.

There were three magistrates, one a chairwoman, tall and thin with sharp, angular features and a brisk, jerky manner, squaring up the papers noisily. Before speaking she eyed Callum up severely over the top of a pair of very large and heavy-looking glasses which had sunk down her nose leaving a permanent dent and some thin, blue, broken veins.

Briskly she explained to the police, his solicitor and to him, that Callum Hughes was charged with attempted murder and that his case would be heard at Shrewsbury Crown Court in due time. In the meantime he was refused bail and would be taken on remand to Stoke Heath Young Offenders' Institute until his case was heard. She advised the police and Stephenson that they should assemble their cases for both defence and prosecution with great care and minimise this first offender's time spent in such uncertainty. Fifteen minutes later it was all over; efficient, brisk and businesslike with a complete absence of emotion.

Shelley was almost breathless with the speed of it all. By ten-thirty her son's immediate fate had been sealed. Callum shot a desperate look at his mother.

She was powerless. There was nothing she could do to help him. He was led from the courtroom.

Wesley Stephenson had set aside a room for her to spend some time alone with her son before his transfer and the minute she entered the dingy room Callum's desperation touched her. He was sitting in the corner, looking out of the window which overlooked a brimming car park full of drivers cruising for a space.

'What'll happen to me, Mum?'

She sat very close to him so she could speak very softly. 'I don't know.'

'How long do you think they'll bang me up for?'

She knew that the slang phrase was his attempt at bravado but instead of reassuring her it had the effect of making her want to cry. The words sounded pathetic coming from his lips. He was not a tough boy. He didn't look one and he couldn't act one and this made her fear for him.

'We'll have to wait and see,' she said. 'If they say what DreadNought was really like maybe it won't be for long.'

'What'll happen to you,' he asked next. 'People'll talk. *You* might have trouble.'

She made an attempt at a smile. 'Now that's one thing I can deal with. I'm used to trouble, Call. Me and trouble are old friends.' The way he looked at her made her think that her attempt at bravado was no more convincing than his.

Paul Talith stuck his head round the door. 'Delays on the Group 4,' he said. 'Van won't be here till late on this afternoon. You can stay till lunchtime, Mrs Hughes, but after that we'll have to take him back to Monkmoor to wait for it.'

She nodded and Talith closed the door.

It was the wrong time now to say that she wished it hadn't happened, that she wished none of it had happened, not the bullying nor the deed itself. Instead she did her best to cheer him up. 'Mr Stephenson says you won't be in for long, Call,' she said. 'He says Stoke Heath's all right.' She made another brave attempt at a smile. 'He says it's quite civilised.' She stretched out one hand to touch his shoulder. 'I'll come and visit you in Stoke Heath. Every week. You'll get sick of the sight of me, Call. I'll bring you things. You'll probably see more of me there than normal. It's not the ends of the earth, is it?' But Callum was staring out of the window at the rows of cars glinting in the September sunshine. His face was frozen.

'What's it going to be like,' he asked, 'not to be able to just walk out of the door and go where you want?'

She couldn't speak.

'What's it like to be locked up every night? To have no choice – no freedom?'

She tried to say something helpful but for once words failed her. There was nothing she could think of to console him.

'Mum', he said desperately, his hands shaking. 'I can't go there. I can't do it. I just can't.'

Shelley glanced at the doorway. Plainly visible were the figures of two policemen. Standing guard. 'There's nothing I can do, Call,' she said.

She was fighting back the tears. Call was right. He did not belong here. She wanted to take him home. For nothing she would have beaten back the guards single-handedly, and taken him away from here. Instead all she had to offer were platitudes. 'Stoke Heath isn't far,' she said again. She tried to laugh. It came out as a bray. 'You'll see too much of me. More than when you're at home. We'll sit and have chats. Talk. Just watch. I'll bring in cigarettes and video games and all sorts of stuff. The time'll fly, Call. It isn't long. Just hang on in there.'

'Why would you bring in fags,' he asked curiously. 'I don't even smoke. I'm not even old enough.'

'Maybe buy you a few pals,' she said. 'I'll bring you in some books as well. They said you can have a telly and a DVD player. Maybe even a computer as well. The time'll pass quick,' she said again. 'Just think what you're going to say when it comes to court. Listen to Mr Stephenson and take all the help you can.'

Her anguish was threatening to engulf her.

'Mum,' he said again urgently, 'you're not pickin' up on me. I can't do it.'

'You haven't got any choice, Call,' she said. 'It's the law. You can't fight that. It's the law.'

But when she watched him being loaded in the back of the

police van she felt as though her control would break. She watched the white van with its high, secure windows, swing out of the car park. One or two reporters held flash cameras high up and tried to catch a picture.

For a while she stood on the court steps, paralysed, watching the spot where the van had left. People passed her by and eyed her curiously. But they were used to dramas being played out on the court steps. No one accosted her.

Finally the doors swung open and Wesley Stephenson came down the steps, two at a time.

'I've been having a talk with the police, Shelley,' he said. 'Callum's a first offender. He's no previous record at all. With a bit of luck – *if* we can persuade some of Roger Gough's gang to testify about the bullying and particularly if the teacher, Mr Farthing, is willing to speak up, he might not be in for long. Let's look on the bright side, and hope that Roger Gough makes a swift and full recovery. If we can expose the bullying they may well reduce the charge to GBH. That's our best chance.'

She managed a watery smile, knowing that Stephenson was doing his very best.

He clapped her on the shoulder and moved on, to his car, out of the car park, home to his family.

Shelley watched bitterly. It was all right for some. She called in at the newsagent's at the bottom of the Lord Hill monument and caught the early edition of the *Shropshire Star.*

Much as she'd expected, she thought.

Call had made the headlines. There was plenty about young thugs and antisocial behaviour. ASBOs were the Government's latest mantra and Hughes, aged thirteen, fitted the bill perfectly. From being an unknown he had become an object of hatred in just a few hours. A meteoric rise to infamy.

Nothing, she noted bitterly, as she scanned down the page, about retaliation, nothing about bullying in schools or the need for some targeted youngsters to protect themselves because no one else would. There was nothing but condemnation. *Unprovoked attack*. The words mocked her from the page. She wanted to set the record straight publicly and knew she might not have the opportunity. She dropped the paper into the bin.

8.30 p.m.

Callum was sick in the back of the truck. He'd always been a bad traveller but the rocking motion together with the confinement on top of the stress all preyed on him so he vomited into a sick bag again and again until his stomach was empty.

The security guard was sympathetic. He handed him a clean bag. 'Get a bit of travel problems myself,' he said. 'Nasty, ain't it?'

Callum eyed him suspiciously. From now on everyone was an enemy.

The sun was sinking behind the horizon by the time they arrived at the main entrance of Stoke Heath. Callum heard the great gates swing open and clang behind him. He heard it echo round and round his head and knew the sound would stay with him even if the place was silent.

Suddenly the doors were flung open and an arc light shone in. Callum stared out. The entire courtyard was floodlit. He would soon learn that no corner was to be left dark. There would be no hiding place; no crevices under stones. Young Offenders' Institutes are not designed to be pleasant places but to confine and re-educate, teach the young hoodlums the error of their ways. On the other hand they are not as intimidating as adult prisons.

The security guards stood up with him and patted him on the back. As Callum stepped out of the van two prison officers stepped forward. The first one, Stevie Matthews, small, plump, with straight, dark hair, was new on the job. This was only her third day. This was her first transfer and her first ever stint of night duty.

Her colleague, however, was a different case altogether. Walton Pembroke, craggy-faced, cynical, a world-weary divorced father of three girls, had thirty years of service behind him. He was one of the old school. Rough and tumble. Shove 'em around a bit. A don't-let-them-have-the-upper-hand sort of a guy. Stevie was learning all the tricks from her senior. Walton Pembroke was a man feared by many. And not just the inmates. Heavy and ponderous, with a beer-drinker's belly and bloodshot blue eyes, he supported the old values. He knew all the tricks of the sly little bastards. He knew where they slipped their drugs, where the beatings happened, what they'd smuggled in via long kisses from their sweethearts or firm handshakes from their mates outside. He knew those that were on the fiddle, those who pushed drugs. He knew the queens and the straight, the sexually predatory and their victims, those who masturbated alone and the ones who cried for their mothers into their pillows at night. He could recognise at thirty paces the racially prejudiced and the oddballs. He could recognise all the breaking points, spot the ones who were likely to erupt at any time. He had seen all sorts of trouble and knew all the warning signs. Those who had been in Stoke Heath more than once anticipated him without relish. He was physically strong, not above taking the odd swipe and he took no shit from any of them. He'd classified Callum Hughes before he'd even stepped out of the security van. Scared wimp. Victim. Mummy's boy. It was written all over the boy's face. He waited until the boy had stumbled a few paces towards him before barking, 'Stand away from me, legs apart. Head up. Now you look at me, son.'

Orders – it was all orders.

Callum looked fearfully into the screw's face.

But I am terrified of Fritz, the hideous, whom I do not hate.

In the same instant that the security van was driving through the gates of Stoke Heath, Martha was turning into the drive of the Albright Hussey, a hotel to eat in when you want to experience luxurious surroundings and good food. Timber-framed with a tall, brick extension built a hundred years after the original, it is on the Ellesmere road out of Shrewsbury, near Battlefield – the site of the bloody conflict between Harry Hotspur and Henry IV in 1404. Modern day Shrewsbury sits comfortably on its history. It was not cheap enough for a young family to eat here regularly so she and Martin had saved it for very special occasions. She parked in front of the half- timbered wing, locked up and pushed the door open.

She was having dinner with a friend. Simon Pendlebury had been an old university friend of Martin's while his wife, Evelyn, had been Martha's friend. Simon had been a mystery to both of them. He was an accountant – or financial advisor whose income seemed to have grown exponentially and inexplicably since he had graduated. Six months ago Evelyn had died of ovarian cancer and since then he had taken to ringing Martha up every now and again and inviting her out to dinner. It was less a romance than a casual friendship with the bond that they had both lost their partners. Martha and Evelyn had been close friends, particularly after Martin's death, and Simon missed her badly. Since losing his wife Simon had grown more sympathetic. Perhaps sensing that she would be missing Sam he had invited her to dinner for her first night after he had gone.

Simon was already standing at the bar, gathering in some menus. He was a tall, dark-haired man with a forceful personality and a direct manner. Martha had often reflected that he had completely dominated his wife. She smiled. Even on such a warm night he was immaculately dressed in a dark suit and sombre, striped tie. He almost always looked as though he belonged in a boardroom. He greeted her with a kiss on the cheek, put his hands on her shoulders and took a long, good look at her before nodding his approval. It seemed he liked the white, beaded skirt and top she had chosen to wear. 'You know, Martha,' he said, handing her a menu and ordering a gin and tonic without asking, 'one thing I like about you is that you're never late.'

'Not to my favourite restaurant, Simon,' she said. 'You might not have waited. You might have started without me.'

'No chance,' he said, passing over the tumbler of gin. 'Now how much tonic?'

'Drown it,' she said. 'I'm thirsty.'

He waited until they had ordered their food before launching into conversation. 'So tell me about Sam,' he prompted.

'You know Sam,' she said. 'He's texted me to say they're sending me some forms to sign.' She grimaced. 'It's probably some horrible disclaimer in case he injures himself.'

'Ouch,' he said, wincing, 'but – you know, Martha, I was thinking as I drove here. I can't say I *do* know Sam – at least not that well. When Evie and I came calling the children were already in bed. I hardly ever met him. And since Martin's died you've always left the children with some *au pair* or other. I haven't seen him for – it must be five years. So no. I don't know Sam.'

'He's football mad,' she said – almost apologetically. 'I don't know where it's come from. Martin wasn't ever like that, was he?'

It was one of the things she valued about Simon's friendship. She could talk to him about Martin – find out about the life her husband had had both before he met her and after, when they were apart. Simon knew things about his friend that she would never know. And this was one of them.

'Actually.' Simon frowned, 'he did play for the varsity team once or twice. In fact he was quite good. Martha.' He put his hand on her arm. 'Do you still miss him very much?'

'Not as much as I did,' she said, almost regretfully. 'I think I'm starting to move on. In fact I know I am. You know, Simon, how I wouldn't change the décor in the study because it reminded me so much of him? The last thing Evie did before she got ill was to help me plan the great redecoration.'

Simon smiled. 'That was Evie,' he said.

'You must miss her.'

'I must, mustn't I?'

It was an odd answer.

And it made Martha think. Although Simon had been Martin's best friend Martin had never quite trusted him. They had shared a flat for years but Martin had puzzled that his flat-mate always seemed to have money – too much money – considering he came from a very deprived family. Simon's father had vanished when he had been a baby and his mother had struggled to raise him and his sister. If Martin had been alive to follow his friend's rise to super-wealth he would have been even more suspicious.

Even more than ten years ago when Martin had still been alive they had felt the poor relations against Simon's ostentatious wealth: the huge house, run by a Philippine couple, the swimming pool and gym block, the daughters at an expensive boarding school, the Rolls Royce and 4X4s, the exotic holidays. After a visit she and Martin would spend most of their journeys home totting up how much the lifestyle cost and how a financial advisor in a modest Shropshire town had built up so much wealth.

They had never found an answer. Evelyn herself had never referred to it and it would have been crass to mention it. Martha had always imagined that one day, her friend would confide in her. But before that day had arrived cancer had claimed her and the secret had gone with her to the grave.

Simon had a very strong personality. He could be opinionated and more than once Martha had locked horns with him. In fact while Martin had been alive Martha had never been quite sure whether she really liked him or not. His charisma was obvious and at times overwhelming but she had seen it switched on and off at will; you could always be guaranteed a lively evening in his company but behind the jokes there had been something ice-cold about him – something inhibiting. But since Martin's death and particularly since his own wife had died Simon Pendlebury appeared to have changed. Perhaps being alone was mellowing him or possibly having achieved so much in his life he was, at last, learning to relax. Towards her he had become warm, sometimes frank and more honest than she would have thought possible. They were characteristics she would never have attributed to him.

So, Simon Pendlebury intrigued her which, in turn, enlivened her so she enjoyed his company.

Maybe one day he would share his secret with her. One day. But how many people have some dark secret buried deep inside their lives and never share it with anyone?

They were summoned to their table and their food arrived.

The two prison warders marched him along the galley and stopped in front of Cell 101. To Callum it seemed deliberate – the association with Room 101. Orwell's Room 101 where people confront their worst fears: spiders, confinement, the dark, heights.

He had a worse fear: that DreadNought would be inside the cell, that he would be locked up for ten hours a night in the same small room as the person he feared most in the world.

Reason told him that DreadNought was in hospital – put there by his trusty, sharpened blade.

But there were other DreadNoughts in the world. Other thugs

and psychopaths, sadists and monsters. And where better to find them than in Room 101 of the Young Offenders' Institute?

Pembroke unlocked the door. In a panic Callum backed against Stevie Matthews but it was Walton Pembroke who shoved him away. 'Watch it.'

Callum was standing in front of a six feet tall, tattooed, shaven-headed bruiser who glared at him.

He tried to escape. 'No way,' he said. 'No way. Don't—'

Pembroke shoved him inside. 'Meet Tyrone Smith,' he said. 'Stoke Heath's answer to Mary Poppins. And this 'ere's Callum Hughes,' he said to Smith. 'on remand. Attempted murder so be careful, won't ya? You and 'im are going to share this luxurious pad for a little while so look after 'im as though he was your brother. Understand?'

Callum tried to escape but Stevie Matthews blocked his way. 'Nervous little bastard, aren't you,' she said lightly. 'Now get in.'

'I can't go in there,' Callum appealed. 'No way,' he said.

'Well you shouldn't have knocked your mate up then, should you?'

'He wasn't my mate.'

'Well – whatever.' Walton Pembroke was losing interest. These first-timers were a nuisance. Namby pamby, wanting their mothers, en suite bathrooms, spoilt brats – most of them. That or so tough you could sharpen a knife on their balls. Streetwise from the age of two. In some ways he'd rather have them like that. At least they took their time on the chin. Not whingeing. He put the suitcase on the floor and moved out of the way.

Time to lock the door.

He flipped open the spyhole. 'Have fun.'

* * *

'Go on, have a dessert.'

Martha shook her head. 'I couldn't possibly. I've no room.'

'Well – if you don't mind, I will. I simply can't resist sticky toffee pudding.'

Martha almost expected him to say it reminded him of boarding school. But of course he couldn't say that, could he? Because he had never been to boarding school, had he? In fact if she recalled correctly what Martin had told her, Simon Pendlebury had gone to school in Bentilee – one of the more deprived areas of Stoke-on-Trent.

She looked across the table at him.

'What are you smiling at, Martha?'

She decided to risk it. 'You,' she said.

'Why?' Even now there was an edge to his voice which made it rasp.

'Because,' she said, 'you are an enigma.'

Callum backed up against the wall and faced his cell mate. Tall, meaty, some foreign blood in him. He was swarthy with big, black eyes which glittered when he eyed him up.

'I'm Tyrone,' he said. 'The screws should have warned you about me.'

'Why?'

'Because. That's why. It's not a good idea to mess with me. I lose my rag, see? I don't like people watchin' me. Nor touchin' me. Understand? And I don't respond too kindly to interference. Understand?'

Callum nodded. Tyrone lifted his head and smiled and Callum felt a moment of pure terror.

Panicked, he looked around the room. It was small. Too

small for them to avoid each other. He retrieved his suitcase and looked up. One of the screws was still watching him through the spyhole, laughing, as though this was a live comedy show. He wanted to beg. He wanted to shout and scream for his mother – even his father, if he'd had any idea who he was. But he didn't. He clamped his mouth shut and closed his eyes.

He heard the spyhole being slid shut, the rattle of keys in locks, the sounds echoing round in his head.

You're losing it, Call, he whispered to himself. Losing it. Losing it.

Tyrone had a podgy, sweating face, large, meaty hands.

'D'ya really kill someone?'

Callum shook his head.

'Botherin' you, was he?'

Callum nodded.

'Do yah wish you 'ad of killed him?'

'Don't know,' he said and felt curiously cold. 'What are you in for?'

'Mind your own...' The meaty fists clenched. Callum closed his eyes, braced himself for the blow – which never came. He would soon learn that Tyrone was unpredictable.

'Burglary,' he said. 'Bastard was in his house all the time. Pretendin' he was out. I knocked 'im about a couple of times.'

'Was he badly hurt?'

Tyrone nodded deliberately and slowly. 'Oh yeah,' he said. 'He was.'

He glanced across at Callum's bag. 'Got any weapons with you?'

Callum shook his head. 'I got some fags though.'

Tyrone jumped to his feet and put his hands around Callum's throat. 'What ya tryin' to do? Kill me slowly?' He put his chin into Callum's face. 'You wouldn't mess with me, would you?'

'No.'

Simon had wolfed down his dessert and they were drinking coffee served with *petit fours* when he returned to the subject of Sam.

'I don't think he's missed me or home life at all,' Martha said. 'And I don't know whether I'm pleased he's finding his independence or a bit hurt that he doesn't appear to be missing me. He texted me to say it was 'ace' and that's about it. As long as he has his beloved football. His only regret is that Michael Owen isn't around any more. And his only fear is that Gerrard will move on. It's taken over his world, Simon. To be honest, in a way, I feel a bit of a failure.'

He smiled at her. 'But you wouldn't want him mother-bound, would you, Martha?'

'No, but...'

'And Sukey?'

'She's happy too. I only hope Agnetha doesn't leave before her Abba craze burns itself out.'

'And so back to you?' he asked finally.

'Oh – I'm OK, Simon.'

He scrutinised her. 'Yes,' he said. 'Just OK. But still missing that spark, I think.'

'Maybe,' she admitted. 'Maybe.' Then she smiled. 'Although sometimes I find it in the most unexpected places.'

'That sounds intriguing.' He waited for her to enlarge but she didn't. She had no intention of leaking her secret alter persona, Martha Rees, Private Sleuth. That was her secret and hers alone. Instead she asked about his daughters.

'Armenia's gone to university,' he said, 'to study accountancy.'

She smiled. 'I hope she's as successful as her father at it.' She raised her glass and met his eyes. Simon returned with one of his inscrutable smiles and she knew he too would give nothing away. So they both had their secrets.

She took a full mouthful of the coffee, leaving it in her mouth and relishing the bitterness before swallowing it. 'I love this place,' she said, looking around.

They both took time out to scan the panelled walls hung with oil portraits of long dead nobility, waxed oak tables, flickering candles. It was luxurious.

Callum welcomed the darkness. He couldn't bear Tyrone to read and despise his fear. He felt tears welling up and sniffed. Immediately Tyrone's hand reached down from the top bunk and fastened round his throat. 'Snivellin' for your mummy, are you?'

'No.'

'You are.' The hand tightened. 'Shut up or I'll give you somethin' to whinge about. Understand? I thump people what bawl.'

'Yeah.'

'Right then. Now give a bloke some peace.'

Shelley was staring out of the window, into the dark night, not caring if anyone was looking in. She had a glass of cheap white wine in her hand and a cigarette in the other although she had given up smoking when she had been expecting

Callum. Neither the wine nor the cigarette was consoling her. From the second of Callum's birth she had always been there for him. Apart from school they had never been parted. And now when he needed her most she could do nothing.

'Martha,' Simon Pendlebury's eyes were locked into hers. 'Have you considered marrying again?'

She shook her head. 'And you?'

'Not yet. It's early days. But I shall.'

She gave him one of her warm smiles. 'Anyone in mind?'

'Not just yet but...' He looked past her out into the restaurant. 'I don't want to stay on my own. That place is too big. Did Evie ever tell you we were thinking of moving?'

This was news to her. 'No.'

'We'd spotted an ancient black and white house a few miles out of Shrewsbury. It's a sixteenth-century manor house. I approached the owners and made them an offer.' Simon Pendlebury gave a mischievous, boyish smile. It made him look very young – almost vulnerable. But not quite.

'An offer he couldn't refuse and he accepted. When Evie was diagnosed I got in touch with him. He said I could still have the place any time over the next year. I have to admit, Martha. I'm tempted.'

'I bet.'

'What about you?'

She shook her head. 'I'm far too comfortable in the White House. I shan't move.'

A young, female violinst was playing very softly in the corner, bent over – almost hunched over her fiddle. She was playing a haunting, Dvorzak gypsy air. Martha listened to it with her usual mix of pleasure and passion. Music should not stir such powerful emotion. And yet it does.

Shelley was still staring out of the window listening to a record. It was from one of the Lloyd-Webber musicals. 'Evita'. 'Where do we go from here?'

It was a question she did not want to answer.

It was completely black in the cell. Callum too was listening to sounds. Doors slamming. Echoing. Cheeky shouts from some of the inmates. A scream. He dared not think what was behind that scream. Muttered curses. The sharp sounds of the screws marching up the walkways, shoving back the spyholes. Another door being opened. A shaft of light as his spyhole was slid back. And slammed closed again.

He needed human contact.

Perhaps he should scream too?

He walked her to her car and kissed her cheek.

'Good night,' he said. 'I'll leave you alone for a few days then I'll be in touch again.'

Still smiling Martha swung out onto the Ellesmere road and accelerated back in towards the town. She fiddled with the car radio and found BBC Radio Shropshire. It was strange but she always had this compulsion to find out what was happening in what she fondly regarded as *her* town before she went to bed. But she had missed the headlines. Instead she heard Krissi Carpenter's voice. 'That was a hit from 1964. Adam Faith singing 'A Message for Martha', written by Burt Bacharach.

And if any Marthas are out there listening this track is being played specially for you.'

Martha was thoughtful as she joined the bypass and swung south towards the woods and the White House.

She had been the focus of some strange and unsettling attention a few months ago – a wreath of flowers left on her doorstep, a dead mouse with a ligature tight around its neck, trees whispering this very song – A Message for Martha. The old '45' had been dumped in her porch.

At first the events had frightened her. She had installed security lights and asked Agnetha to be careful that she always activated the burglar alarm and kept the safety chain fastened when she was in the house alone. She had suspected that the perpetrator must be connected with a case which the family had felt had resulted in an unsatisfactory verdict but although she racked her brains she had come up with nothing. Lately there had been no ghostly contacts and she had begun to believe that the person who taunted her had played out his or her vengeance.

She hoped so.

The hit still seemed personal.

The house was shrouded in darkness as she locked her car door. Agnetha and Sukey must be asleep.

And for that she was glad.

Shelley was on her fourth glass of wine and her fifth cigarette.

And Callum?

Was not asleep.

CHAPTER FOUR

Thursday 8th September, 6.58 a.m.

Martha woke early to an uneasy feeling. It took her seconds to locate the cause.

The phone was ringing.

She picked it up, glanced at the radio alarm. It was early, a little before seven. Already she knew it would hardly be good news and she was right. The voice was formal. 'Martha Gunn? It's Alex Randall here. Bad news, I'm afraid. We've got a death in custody.'

Inwardly she groaned. This was the beginning of the worst. Enquiries, allegations of police brutality, foul play.

'Give me the details, Alex. Where did it happen? At the prison?'

'No. Stoke Heath. A young lad. Thirteen. His name was Callum Hughes. He was a Shrewsbury lad. Up in front of the magistrates yesterday morning on a charge of attempted murder. You may have heard of the case. It made the headlines. He stabbed a classmate outside school. He was put on remand yesterday morning and transferred to Stoke Heath.' Alex gave a deep sigh. 'It looks like he hanged himself in his cell, Martha.'

'Oh no.' Every time she imagined herself inured to her job something like this happened.

'I saw him myself the day before yesterday when he was brought in. Frightened rabbit of a boy. With his mother. Martha – he was only thirteen. First time offender.'

So it had touched DI Randall too.

'I'll call in to Stoke Heath in an hour or two. Do you want to move the body?'

'Yes. Mark's done a swift examination and he's happy for us to take it down to the morgue – if that's all right with you. I'm just on my way to break the news to his mother. I feel as the Senior Investigating Officer I at least owe her that.'

'I don't envy you.'

'Part of the job, Martha.'

'OK then, Alex. I'll talk to you later.' So much for a lie-in and a cup of freshly brewed coffee.

Shelley hadn't slept either but lain with an advancing headache, suspended somewhere between waking and sleeping, soberness and a hangover, day and night. She too was woken early in the morning, not by a telephone ringing but by hammering on the door. And like the hammering two days ago she knew it portended bad news. She was beginning to learn: no one except the police knocked on doors so hard or so early in the morning. She allowed herself the luxury of lying still for what she feared would be her last moment of peace. Something was very wrong. Ideas flashed through her mind as she tied her dressing gown around her waist and descended the stairs. Maybe DreadNought had died in the night. Perhaps, oh Heavens above, they had decided to let her son go. And that was him, banging at the door.

By the time she reached the bottom step she was not sleepy any more but a hopeful, yet fearful automaton, watching herself go through the movements of shooting back the bolt, turning round the key, pulling open the door which always stuck. The faces which met hers were grim.

'Mrs Hughes?'

It was the tall policeman with the craggy face and nice eyes. But his eyes looked at her differently now. They met hers with pity and an apology. Behind him hovered an awkward WPC. Shelley Hughes brushed the hair out of her eyes. 'Callum?' she said, clutching the doorframe because the dizziness threatened to send her reeling.

'May we come in?'

She knew it was a bad sign. It was *all* a bad sign. She nodded and backed along the narrow hallway.

They followed her into the lounge and waited for her to sit down.

Another bad sign.

'I'm afraid there's been an accident.'

She looked from one to the other, her head turning without any conscious movement, gliding over her neck. 'What sort of accident?' Her voice was harsh and gravelly. Hostile.

'It's your son.' The eyes met hers fearlessly and with honesty now. She stared back at him, waiting. Waiting. Not hoping any more.

'Mrs Hughes, I'm sorry. It appears that he's committed suicide.'

She stared, uncomprehending.

'He hanged himself in his cell some time during the night.'

She could feel herself sinking into oblivion, straight down into the black spiral of her worst nightmare.

'You're telling me he's dead?'

Alex Randall nodded.

'Weren't you watching him?'

'Not enough – obviously.'

'You let him do this – when you knew he was terrified of being inside?'

The policeman nodded again. 'There will be an enquiry.'

And these words made her anger erupt. 'An enquiry? A fucking enquiry? Oh well, that's OK then. An enquiry'll solve everything, won't it? Fine. Just great. My son hangs himself in your care and you tell me there'll be an enquiry?' She dropped her head on her arms and submitted to great, wracking sobs.

Inspector Randall stood up then. 'Do you want us to take you to see him?'

Martha padded downstairs to make the coffee, taking it back to the bedroom with her to cool. It was seven o'clock. She took a quick shower first then drank the cooling coffee. Agnetha would have to walk Bobby this morning. She wanted to get to Stoke Heath in good time. The wheels must crank into motion. Mark Sullivan would be in touch later, after the boy's mother had identified him. He would want to proceed with the post-mortem as soon as possible. Her day was filling up.

Agnetha and Sukey staggered downstairs minutes later, both brushing long blonde hair out of their eyes. Agnetha was the more awake. 'Good morning, Mrs Gunn. I hope you had a good evening last night with your friend.' Agnetha, in baby-doll pyjamas, gave her a sly wink.

'I did, thank you, Agnetha. Morning, Sukey.'

'Hello, Mum.' Sukey gave her a sleepy kiss, putting her arms around her. 'How's things?'

'OK.' Martha had never involved her children in her work. Having lost their father it was hardly necessary to remind either of them about the consequences of mortality. It was there, staring down at them from the mantelpiece every day of their young lives. She didn't want them to think too much about death.

'How's your new class, Sukes?'

'OK.' Sukey was winding a lock of hair around her finger so Martha knew she wanted to ask something. She watched her and picked up on some of the agitation. But Sukey was not to be hurried. She eyed Martha's grey work-suit with undisguised distaste. 'Are you off to work?'

Martha nodded.

'What time'll you be home, Mum?'

'Darling – I can't say.'

Sukey nodded then tugged Agnetha by the hand. 'Come on. I want you to braid my hair.'

They both skipped out of the room and Martha felt a sudden pang.

In concentrating on providing I have failed both my children.

She started up her car and headed towards the bypass. Stoke Heath is to the north-east of Shrewsbury, an easy twenty-minute drive starting on the Shrewsbury bypass, fanning out along the A53 towards the Potteries and then a right turn at

Tern Hill Barracks, south, down the A41 in the direction of Wolverhampton. Stoke Heath Young Offenders' Institute is a little way down, on the right hand side. You cannot miss it. High fences, flood lighting throughout the hours of dusk and darkness, numerous road signs to guide in the relatives who travel, sometimes from far away.

Martha was tuned in to the local news station. The news was of the financial problems at the Royal Shrewsbury Hospital and the report of a horrific car crash along one of the many country roads. The news hadn't broken yet. When it did it would soon take over the headlines.

It is not strictly speaking necessary for a coroner to visit the scene of the crime but Martha knew, from experience, that mere computer simulations were never as good as the real thing. In a case such as this, actually *seeing* the room in which the suicide had occurred was invaluable. This would be a high profile case with numerous enquiries to follow. She would need to have a clear picture of what had happened.

When Jericho, her assistant, rang her at a little after eight on her car phone she took malicious delight in telling him that she knew about the suicide and was already on her way to Stoke Heath. 'Well,' he said, miffed, 'why didn't they inform me?'

She took pity on him. 'Detective Inspector Randall rang me just before seven,' she explained. 'I don't suppose he thought you'd be in the office so early.'

She was smiling as she spoke, thankful she and Jericho did not have a video link. But she knew that Jericho was as reliable as the BBC one o'clock pips. He always arrived at eight am. Not before.

He was mollified. 'Well Doctor Sullivan's been on the line and I didn't know anything about it. He wants to know when he can do the post-mortem.'

'Ring him back, Jericho, can you? I'm driving. I'm going to be in Stoke Heath until late morning then I'd better call in on you. Tell him some time this afternoon would be best.'

There was a pause. She pictured him scratching his grey pate to find some fact he knew which she so far did not. Then he cleared his throat. 'The deceased's name is Callum Hughes,' he said importantly. 'And the next of kin has been informed.'

She had to hand it to him. 'Thank you, Jerry,' she said politely. 'Who is his next of kin?'

'His mother. She lives in Harlescott. She's identifying him now.'

'Poor woman,' she said.

Poor woman, she thought. *Poor woman. On one day she learns her son has stabbed another boy. The next she is at the magistrate's court. And on the third she learns that he is dead by his own hand. Poor woman.*

'Yes,' he agreed and rung off.

Martha had reached Stoke Heath. She pulled onto the small car park set aside for visitors and approached the front door.

It was not the first time that she had been here and she had always been surprised that she was so sensitive to this place and its atmosphere. A naughty boys' correction centre with the underlying flavour of prison.

They were expecting her. The two prison guards who had been on night duty were hanging on in a small ante-room.

They would already have been questioned by the police. As she was signed in a familiar tall figure walked through the door.

'Alex,' she said. 'You're still here.'

His eyes lit up. 'I'm so glad you came out, Martha,' he said. 'We didn't expect you for another half hour.'

'The traffic was light and you woke me early.'

'Sorry,' he said, still smiling. And there was not a hint of an apology in his voice. He looked around him at the watching guards, a few police officers and the very public corridor. 'Is there somewhere private we can talk?'

He led her to a room at the side of the main hatch, Martha aware, all the time, that the beady eye of CCTV was following their every move along the corridor.

They sat down in scruffy, red armchairs, either side of a scratched pine coffee table. This was obviously an interview room for the relatives.

'So?'

Alex's eyes were intelligent, perceptive, hazel-tinged and curiously sharp.

'The deceased is a lad named Callum Hughes. Thirteen years old. No sign of Dad. Lives with Mum up towards Harlescott in a small, privately-owned semi-detached. She works as a cleaner in a local office block. On Tuesday afternoon Callum assaulted a classmate, Roger Gough, outside the school. Stabbed him once in the chest with a knife. Gough is currently at the Royal Shrewsbury Hospital with a collapsed lung. He's not in any danger but he's pretty uncomfortable.'

'Just stop there a minute, Alex. Right or left lung?'

'Left.'

'How near the heart?'

He held up his hand, his finger and his thumb one inch apart. Martha winced.

'Had Callum ever used a knife before?'

Alex shook his head.

'Had he ever threatened this boy before?'

Another shake of the head.

'Did he have a record of criminal activity?'

'No.'

'So are you saying that a perfectly normal schoolboy with absolutely no record whatsoever of previous violence took out a knife and without provocation stabbed a schoolmate an inch from the heart?'

'That's about it.'

She watched his face. 'And?' she prompted.

'He bought the knife specifically for the purpose a couple of weeks ago – just before the schools went back.'

She waited.

'At the same time as he bought the knife he also bought a sharpening stone. We could see the marks on the knife where he'd used it. I think it was that that made us charge him with attempted murder rather than GBH. There was no question of bail for the lad.'

She nodded. She could see the logic behind this. 'Did he offer any explanation?'

'He was fairly shocked by it all. He said very little.'

'Yet he must have planned something. Did you ask that question?'

Alex gave a tired smile and she remembered that he would

have been up from first light. Deaths in custody were always bad news – particularly when the victim was a first offender and a minor. It made the prison service appear uncivilised. Monstrous. One offence and you died?

'Did you get *any* sort of explanation?'

'His mother made allegations that Gough had been bullying her son.'

'What do you think, Alex? Are we looking at a potential killer? Or a young boy trying to defend himself?'

Alex sighed. 'I don't know. By all accounts on Tuesday it was a completely unprovoked attack. I didn't know last night what sort of person Callum was. I just couldn't make up my mind. One minute he looked like a no-hoper then next it all fitted. He was a violent villain. And yet, Martha, his mother is a pleasant, decent sort of a woman. And he seemed a decent sort of boy. Their claims hung together even though there was no corroboration. None of the boys' schoolmates have confirmed the bullying story.'

'And the boy he stabbed?'

'I'd only seen Roger Gough when he was in agony having all sorts done to him in the hospital. I could imagine him being a bully whereas Hughes appeared a frightened rabbit. A very scared and very young boy. Gough must have been twice the weight of Callum Hughes. If he'd wanted to bully him he could easily have done it – particularly with a cheering gang around.'

'A cheering gang? Then why haven't any of them come forward? Surely young Callum must have had *some* friends, *someone* to speak up for him?'

'Not so far.'

Martha knew what they were both doing. Not questioning Callum Hughes's suicide at all but looking into his state of mind as he had committed the act.

'And now Callum Hughes is dead.'

Alex nodded.

'So wind me on to last night,' she said. 'I take it he was in front of the magistrate yesterday?'

'Yes.'

'And arrived here?'

'Late afternoon in one of the vans.'

'You'll want to speak to the security guards who sat in the back with him.'

Alex nodded again.

'So he was brought here. Was he judged a suicide risk?'

Alex's eyes met hers for a moment. His frown deepened. 'To some extent they *all* are here,' he said. 'They're all little boys frightened of what's going to happen to them. Those that come from good homes – and they're in the minority – are frightened of physical violence. The others – well – they're all too used to it. But it doesn't make things any easier. And, Martha, the prison officers can't protect the inmates all the time. They can't be everywhere twenty-four-seven. It simply isn't possible. With so many youths clustered together there are bound to be incidents.'

For some reason Martha's mind flashed to her own son. Sam. There were plenty of young, active youths in the Liverpool Academy. Were there incidents there too? Were there? Could they be prevented? What was happening to him? Text messages tell you so very little. *Things are hotting up,* had been the last one, with a tacked on, *Hope Bobby is fine.*

She must go and see him, satisfy herself that he was well and happy.

'I sense you have more to tell me, Alex.'

Again Alex Randall looked deeply troubled. 'Callum was, unfortunately, put in a cell with a complete psychopath,' he said, his jaw tight and angry, his mouth pressed into a thin gash. 'Tyrone Smith is vicious and unpredictable.' His eyes gleamed briefly. '*I* wouldn't fancy being locked in a small room, through the hours of darkness, with him.'

'What are you suggesting?'

Alex looked uncomfortable. 'Callum Hughes was put into his cell at 10 p.m. last night. The night duty officers actually went into the cell at eleven and at midnight and everything seemed fine. They say that Callum was sleeping, Smith too. They left and locked up. The next thing they knew it was six-thirty in the morning and they found him slumped on the floor, a ligature round his neck, which had been looped round the bed. He was quite cold. The assumption was that he'd been faking his sleep and had hanged himself soon after the second visit of the officers.'

'Why? I don't understand what you're saying. Are you suggesting that Smith had a hand in his death?'

'No – but, he was the wrong cell mate. Tyrone Smith is fifteen years old. He's six feet tall. Half Afro-Caribbean and half Liverpudlian. His mother was a prostitute. His father is a complete unknown. Almost certainly one of the drug dealers she consorted with. I tell you, Martha, that guy has lived in places we wouldn't even visit in our nastiest nightmares. He was in for a long stretch for a brutal, armed burglary. He blinded the occupant of the house by sticking a knife through his eye. The guy was lucky to live but he lost his eye and will never sleep easy again. It was a terrible crime. Tyrone Smith always worked alone. He was a loner, a dangerous loner with no friends. Barred from school at six years old, in and out of institutions. The man was seventy-six years old, elderly and harmless. Smith could simply have robbed him and left. There was no need for that level of violence. He simply enjoyed it. Tyrone Smith is one of those characters born to offend.'

Martha was picking up on the reason behind this interview. 'And Hughes – who was arguably defending himself against another such type – was locked in a cell for eight and a half hours with this guy?'

Randall nodded.

'You can almost understand his thought processes,' Martha said. 'He would have got sent down for how long?'

'He'd have got a couple of years. The defence would have gathered up a couple of character witnesses. They may even have hit lucky with some corroboration of the bullying story but with the evidence of the sharpened knife deliberately placed in his schoolbag you can't duck out of the premeditation charge. He would definitely have got a custodial sentence and he knew it. Look at it this way, Martha,' Alex appealed. 'We can't have youths armed like that roaming the streets. Quite apart from the issue of public safety there is the issue of sending out messages to other would-be offenders. Give a good enough reason and you get away with murder. We *have* to protect the public. It's what we're here for. Callum Hughes *had* to be locked away. Anything else would have made a mockery of our justice system.'

82   PRISCILLA MASTERS

'So what did he use?'

Alex Randall looked uncomfortable. 'Tyrone Smith, being in for a long stretch, was allowed certain privileges.'

Martha raised her eyebrows.

'He had a computer. Not linked to the Internet. Just to play games on. While Tyrone Smith was *apparently* sleeping the sleep of the innocent Callum unloosed a length of computer cable, looped it around the bed end and hanged himself. When the warders unlocked the door in the morning Callum was well – dead and Smith was still asleep. Delyth Fontaine said Hughes was quite cold when she attended at a quarter to seven and Mark agreed that he'd been dead for a good few hours. Resuscitation was out of the question.'

'Wasn't he on an hourly watch?'

Alex Randall shook his head.

'Did no one go in his cell to check later?'

Again Alex looked uneasy. 'We've already interviewed the two warders at some length. They say they didn't go in after midnight. They looked in through the spyhole but all seemed quiet and they thought it better not to disturb him.'

'So what's bothering you, Alex?'

'Your antennae,' he said, 'awesome.'

She waited.

'It's nothing,' he said. 'Nothing really.'

'Except?'

'It really is nothing. It's just *opportune*. There's a victim. And Callum Hughes *was* a victim. He had it written all over him. Skinny, frightened-looking, no confidence, that horrible sag these youngsters have in their shoulders. He was inviting people to pick on him. So there is he and there is Tyrone

Smith, a psychopath, who's always on the lookout for a victim.'

'Are you suggesting Tyrone Smith incited Hughes to hang himself?'

'No. He wasn't clever enough to do that.'

'Intimidated him then?'

Randall's expression was pained. 'I can't prove it,' he began awkwardly. 'I don't know. And what difference would it make?'

'Maybe a great deal – to his mother.'

'But then what? Would it make the prison service culpable for mixing and matching inmates?'

'Alex,' she said softly. 'Whatever the cost we must find out the truth. We owe it to this boy and to justice.'

'Well then – in that case – we must make sure that Mark Sullivan does a thorough post-mortem.'

'Should I be speaking to the prison officers?'

Alex rubbed the back of his neck. 'I'd quite like to start that off first,' he said. 'If I can get to the bottom of it on my own I'd feel happier. I can ask whether Smith has ever assaulted anyone before. I have to say, Martha, I'd be very surprised if he hadn't.'

Martha nodded.

'I'd better take a look round the cell,' she said. 'That's what I came for. I take it Tyrone Smith's been moved elsewhere?'

'Of course.'

They walked along the corridor, a prison officer locking and unlocking the doors in front and behind them.

It was a small, crowded, claustrophobic room, painted cream, a sink and a toilet (without a seat) at the far end beneath a frosted window. On the right side were bunks stripped down to the bedsprings. The police had removed all the bedding and the mattresses. The window had been opened an inch or two but there was still the sour scent of stale vomit.

Tyrone Smith had made his temporary home quite comfortable with a computer, stacks of games, pin-ups of women with impossibly large breasts and strangest of all a magazine picture of a giant four-tiered beefburger complete with bright red relish. Martha studied the picture with interest.

Alex pointed to some tape on the side of the bed frame of the upper bunk. 'Hughes was in the lower bunk,' he said, 'Smith in the upper one. He had been sharing with a youth called Gavin Morrison but he's been moved nearer London so his family can visit.'

'It might be an idea if you interviewed Gavin Morrison,' she said, 'and asked him what sort of a cell mate Tyrone Smith made.'

She looked round the room and saw a pair of shoes, neatly paired, side by side. Reebok trainers.

Sam had an identical pair.

Suddenly overcome with claustrophobia she turned around. She had seen enough. She felt a desperation to escape, to get of here.

Had Callum Hughes felt like that too?

She left Stoke Heath soon after. The police could deal with the remaining interviews. She had a few hours' paperwork before attending the post-mortem this afternoon.

The news must have leaked out. At the gates of Stoke Heath someone had laid a wreath of flowers. Red and white carnations. Liverpool colours. And the mantra, *Callum, you'll never walk alone.*

It seemed that Callum Hughes and her son shared the same passion for a football club.

Jericho was waiting for her when she entered her office. Though he was unsuitable as a coroner's assistant, being a shocking gossip, he was, in other ways, extremely efficient. 'The post-mortem's at two o'clock,' he said. 'I'm to let them know if you're wantin' to attend and if the time is inconvenient.'

'It's fine,' she said and wandered through to her office.

Her post had been opened and the letters requiring her attention laid to one side. Junk mail had already been binned and the second pile contained letters which could be dealt with at her leisure.

'And how are things at Stoke Heath?'

'Rather unpleasant at the moment.'

'The young lad that knifed someone a couple of days ago?' She nodded.

'Hah,' he said, pleased. 'I *thought* it was the same boy. Nasty piece of work. Sharpened the knife, I heard.'

She felt she should defend the dead boy but Jericho didn't give her the chance. 'How did he do it?'

'We don't know for definite yet,' she said pointedly. 'The post-mortem's this afternoon. But,' she yielded to Jericho's bright, curious expression, 'it looks as though he hanged himself.'

'Ah – these lads,' he said with regret. 'They will do it. Coffee now, Mrs Gunn?'

'Thanks.' As Jericho left she reflected how his hair was so

badly cut she wondered whether he did it himself. Grizzly grey, uneven, prone to sticking out in all directions, which made her cross to the mirror and take stock of her own hair. It too needed a cut. And that meant running the gauntlet of Vernon Grubb's scrutiny. As usual she decided it would have to be put off till next week. This week was simply too busy.

She glanced at the letter on top of the pile. It was handwritten in quite an untidy, scrawling hand. When she had read it through twice she called in Jericho. 'Where did this come from?'

He started rifling through the bin. 'Don't know. Is it important? Hah.' He emerged with a white envelope. 'It came in this.'

She snatched it from him. It bore a first class stamp and had a Shrewsbury postmark. Aware that Jericho was watching her without bothering to disguise his curiosity she put the envelope in her handbag together with the letter.

'Is everything all right, Mrs Gunn?'

No. It wasn't. He was here again, her ghostly haunter.

Hello, Martha, she could almost hear the voice which had whispered to her through the trees last winter, *I am here again to make sure you remember. I do have a message for you. In time I will deliver it. Be patient.*

She should give the letter to Alex. Let the police sort it out.

CHAPTER FIVE

Martha didn't always attend post-mortems. She wouldn't have had the time. But this case would attract a great deal of media attention. Callum Hughes had been young; the schoolboy stabbing had been his first offence and his suicide had occurred within twenty-four hours of his detention. There was plenty of material for a Press feeding frenzy. The other reason that she had decided to attend today's post-mortem was that it was easier to conduct an inquest when she had watched, first hand, the pathologist reach his decision. So she drove to the mortuary.

But she almost groaned out loud when she walked in and caught her first sight of Mark Sullivan for a couple of months. She had spoken to him a few times recently and he had sounded fine but words across a telephone line give you little idea of what state a person is in.

He moved towards her unsteadily. 'Martha,' he said.

Alex Randall was standing behind him, concern etching new lines in his craggy face.

He met her eyes. And unaccountably Martha felt angry. Mark Sullivan *knew* that this post-mortem would be important. The skinny, small corpse lying on the slab was not a little old lady who had died of natural causes in a nursing home. This was the suspicious and controversial death of a youth who should have lived for many more years. This was somebody's child. The evidence the pathologist uncovered would be exposed to a court of law. There was a feeling that it was important that deaths in custody were aired right out in the open or murmurings were soon born. Failing justice, truth, the integrity of the entire British legal system. Everything they all stood for and held dear relied on this tissue evidence that Mark Sullivan was due to retrieve. And he had been drinking.

She and Alex exchanged a quick nod.

'Have we time for a coffee?'

Sullivan looked bemused. 'Coffee?'

'Yes. A black coffee,' Martha said firmly. Had Sullivan been a little more sober he would have picked up on the acid in her tone and known she was aware that he was too drunk to perform a post-mortem requiring any but the most basic of skills.

Sullivan shrugged. 'OK. If you like.'

They filed into his office and Martha held back to speak to Alex. 'Has the boy's mother formally identified him?'

'Yes.'

'How was she?'

He shook his head. 'Distraught. How would you feel?'

She didn't even want to contemplate.

Mark Sullivan visibly improved after two mugs of strong coffee. Twenty minutes later he stood up and smiled. 'Right then.'

As they filed back into the post-mortem room neither Martha nor Alex said anything. It was better that Sullivan approached this case with an open mind.

Post-mortems follow a rigid protocol. After the corpse has been stripped, Alex and another officer bagged up the clothes. Evidence: a pair of shorts and a T-shirt. Obviously, like most teenagers, Callum Hughes did not wear pyjamas. She blinked away the vision of Sam stumping around the kitchen in similar clothes, scratching around for something to eat. As the mortician and Randall measured the youth's crown rump measurement and weighed him Martha reflected how thin the lad had been. There was none of the tough wiriness of her son.

Stop doing this, she told herself. Stop comparing. This is not Sam but someone else's son, the only link being their age. They were born in the same year. That is all.

Her eyes dropped downwards. This boy stabbed another. Maybe it was through desperation, maybe malice, but he is not Sam.

She turned her attention full on Mark Sullivan and reflected. He might have been teetering on the edge of alcoholism but he was still a competent pathologist.

He studied the boy's face first, fingered a mark around the right eye socket, another, smaller one on the left brow and a third on the upper cheek. He touched a large bruise on the right shin then stood back for a while, frowning, finally crossing the room to study the police photographs pinned up on the board.

'When he was found,' he asked Alex Randall, 'the back of his head was against the bed, wasn't it?'

Both Martha and Alex nodded. 'I wonder if the body could have twisted,' he said. 'These look as though they were sustained at around the time of death. I don't suppose anyone could verify?'

'His cell mate slept all the way through.'

Mark Sullivan's eyebrows rose almost to his hairline but he made no comment.

He still said nothing as he severed the computer lead from around the boy's neck, preserving the knot with great care. He handed it to the WPC who had accompanied Randall. She put it in a bag.

'You might think to speak to the prison warders, Alex,' he said. 'Just check about the length of the cable to ascertain whether it was long enough to have allowed him much movement.' His eyes drifted back to the boy's face and Martha knew he was unhappy about the injuries. This puzzled her because she could see they were not serious; they had played no part in his death. But this was something she had noticed about pathologists. They like to be able to explain every lesion – no matter how small.

Randall nodded and looked down at his notes. '"When he was found",' he quoted, '"he was slumped against the side of the bed, the flex looped and knotted on the baseboard which is latticed wire. There wasn't much slack"'. He looked up. 'I can't see him turning around myself and hitting his face on the edge of the bed but if he was standing up then dropped I suppose it's a possibility. Theoretically,' he added as an afterthought.

Sullivan met his eyes, looked at Martha, inviting a comment but neither of them said anything. So Mark Sullivan turned his attention back to the brain, his concentration deepening as he became absorbed. Martha understood that as the neck contained the vital evidence in a suicidal hanging the area had to be clear of blood. She noticed too that as Sullivan worked his hands steadied and his eyes cleared. Now his concentration was total. Periodically he glanced back at the police photographs which were pinned up on an x-ray board but apart from that he was quite still – except for his hands.

Now it was time to study the mark the computer lead had left. Narrow and well defined, brownish in colour with a tinge of blue at its edge and a leathery consistency to the skin. No need for Sullivan to point out the congested blood vessels above the V-shaped impression which was just above the larynx and extended almost to the boy's ears.

Sullivan began to slice through the tissues, working as delicately as an artist as he peeled back the layers of the boy's throat. Martha watched him, mesmerised. She had to hand it to Mark Sullivan – he had a uniquely dextrous skill. Maybe if he hadn't liked his bottle so much he might have become a Professor in Pathology and trained students to work as perfectly as he did. He would have been able to make a real and permanent contribution to the science. As it was he had buried himself away from academia and the hub of a university career and dived into the nearest bottle neck. Again Martha felt that sudden wash of anger at the mess he was making of his life.

To cover her emotion she wandered towards the photographs herself and was again struck by how thin Callum Hughes had been. He had been underdeveloped, small for his age. Boys of thirteen vary hugely in the stages of their development. But she couldn't help reflecting that his size had contributed to the bullying and the bullying had led to the assault and so on to his suicide. How cruel nature can be.

Once Mark had finished examining the neck he opened the

chest and for a while his fingers probed various orifices. Neither Alex nor Martha spoke. They didn't want to break the pathologist's concentration. A couple of times Mark spoke into a small Dictaphone making audio-notes as he worked. Once he looked up. 'By the way,' he said, 'there were some contusions on the ribs so I did a couple of x-rays. There was an old fracture.'

Alex and Martha exchanged glances. It was the first concrete corroboration of Callum and Shelley's story.

'Any idea how old,' Martha asked casually.

'Oh, somewhere under a year.'

His attention had moved on.

The liver, brain, spleen and heart were weighed.

He moved to the leg wound, measuring the bruise, exploring the tissues beneath, his frown deepening as he worked, some of his attention obviously trying to piece together Callum's final hours.

She waited for him to finish, peel off his gloves, throw his operating gown into the laundry bin and wash up while the mortuary assistant finished the stitching up.

But Sullivan was pondering. He deliberated over the actions, performing them like an automaton, obviously working his way through all that he had seen, delaying the moment when he would have to present his findings to coroner and police. Even behind his glasses she could read troubled abstraction in his eyes. Something was bothering him.

'Shall we...?' He led them back into his office and deliberately closed the door behind them.

'What is it, Mark?'

Sullivan cleared his throat. To his side Alex Randall stood, almost quivering with attention.

'Martha,' he finally appealed. 'You know as well as I do that medicine isn't always an exact science.'

She nodded.

'I have a conflict here,' he said. 'It's easy for a pathologist to extrapolate too much from the PM. And I can't be absolutely sure.'

'Of what exactly?'

'Well – put it this way. There were definite bruises on the face.'

Both Martha and Alex nodded their agreement. They'd seen them.

'I don't know whether he could have twisted at some point to cause the facial bruising.'

Martha and Alex waited.

'The trouble is that the edge of the bunk is metal. Quite sharp. Obviously sharp objects tend to give a different injury from a blunt one. The bruising on the face was not done by a sharp, metallic object unless the bedding was covering it at the time of impact.'

Sullivan continued.

'The same goes for the injury to the occiput which looks as though he fell backwards from standing. And as for the shin injury – I can't see that being caused by the same impact. It's so much more severe than the other injuries. I think it was a kick sustained a few hours before he died.'

Sullivan eyed Randall. 'You could ask the prison warders whether they moved the bedding.' Randall nodded.

'It could explain the injuries as all being caused at the time of hanging although…' Sullivan's eyes drifted round the room.

'I take it there was no resisting arrest?'

Randall shook his head. 'Does he look the sort of guy who could resist a couple of six foot PCs?'

They all shook their heads.

'So what are you saying, Mark?' Martha asked.

'Well. The cause of death was hypoxia due to asphyxia. That's all I can say with certainty.'

'You mean the ligature round the neck?'

'Was almost certainly the cause of the asphyxia. I'll put it more clearly. He died from the hanging and not from the other more minor injuries. But there is evidence of assault.'

'Almost certainly? What are you saying, Mark? That it's a potential *homicide?*' Randall was frowning.

'No.' Sullivan's tone was still careful. 'I'm saying that I know what the cause of death is. What I don't know are the circumstances that led up to the asphyxia. I don't know how to explain all the injuries – even the minor ones on his face and on the back of his head. Put it like this. I'd prefer it if they weren't there. Maybe there's a simple explanation. It's possible that his cell mate knocked him about a bit. Look, Alex,' he appealed, 'too many pathologists go for dogmatic statements that they're in no position to make. I'm just saying what can be borne out by science. That's all. And we can't ignore the shin injury which was delivered with some force. He could have knocked against something – maybe the transfer van went too fast round a corner and he fell off his seat. It could explain the occipital bruising and even the shin injury but it's probable that someone kicked him. Hard. It's a typical footballer's injury if they're not wearing shin guards.'

Martha winced.

Mark Sullivan continued. 'All I'm saying, Alex, is that you probably need to ask the prison warders a few things. Clarify matters. That's all. I'm not pointing a finger of suspicion. We all want the same – surely?' He glanced briefly at both their faces. 'To be sure that we reach the right verdict.'

Alex's frown deepened. 'This is turning out to be even more tricky than I initially thought,' he said. 'I thought I was just up against a criticism from the more liberal members of our society for our penal system. What you're giving me is a mystery.'

'Forensics may be a science,' Mark countered. 'But it isn't always as exact as we might wish.'

Alex gave a deep sigh. 'How can we conduct an enquiry if we don't even know what happened?'

'Well – whatever,' Martha said briskly, 'I think it would be a good idea if I spoke to the boy's mother this afternoon. The earlier the better. I'll open the inquest next week and we can adjourn it pending police enquiries.'

'I suppose so,' Alex said reluctantly, 'though I'd have loved closure. But if you're not happy, Mark?'

They both knew he was inviting Sullivan to modify his verdict and they also knew that Sullivan wouldn't do that, never had done it. He took some time to reach his conclusion but once he had he would stick to it. In fact his pedantic nature was one of the ingredients that had earned him their respect. Counter-balanced by his drinking habits.

The three of them exchanged looks. Martha voiced their thoughts. 'I don't need to remind you. Not a word of this goes outside here. If the Press get even a sniff of it all sorts of allegations of brutality and cover-ups will emerge. I'll tell his mother that we need to do further tests and that you, Alex, are going to be interviewing people at the prison as well as the arresting officers. This is very sensitive information. For the time being we can be non-committal.'

Her eyes drifted around the room, from the stark photographs to the corpse. 'I don't want this young lad buried until we are as certain as we can be of all the circumstances that led up to his death.'

She thanked Sullivan and they left the mortuary. She caught up with Randall outside. 'Alex, how are you?'

He gave her one of the rare smiles that transformed his face. 'I'm not bad – considering this.' He jerked his head back towards the morgue. 'Bit of a shame, really, that Sullivan wasn't willing to be more dogmatic.'

'You can't expect him to compromise his science.'

'No. But those bruises will cost a lot of police hours – and I bet you a dinner at your favourite restaurant that the verdict is the same. The poor lad simply couldn't hack it. He panicked and ended it all. The bruising on the head, the face and the shin will turn out to be an irrelevance.'

Or a vital clue?

She nodded. 'It'll be worth a dinner to have a simple verdict of suicide. By the way,' she added, 'how's the lad that he stabbed?'

'He's having a bit of a battle. Had some sort of complications. You know what doctors are like – born pessimists and as elusive as a virgin. They're being cagey but giving out some dark hints such as – 'not as well as we'd expected'. His parents are spending all their time at the hospital so draw your conclusions from that,' Alex said.

'*C'est la vie et mort.*'

They exchanged a few more pleasantries and Martha climbed into her car. It was as she was letting the clutch out that she wondered what Randall had meant – considering? Not bad – considering? Had he been referring to the Callum Hughes case or something else? Once she had referred to his personal life. She knew he was married. But response to friendly questions had caused him pain so she had buried the subject – permanently.

She mused the point for a while before turning her mobile phone back on. One message, and a text from Sam. She turned to the text first.

Hello, Mum. I need to talk 2 u. Can u ring me at 6. How's Bobby? Hope he's not catching 2 many mice.

She read it through and sensed the anxiety that lay behind it. What was wrong?

Mother-like she was already worrying.

Next she listened to Jericho Palfreyman's slow tones informing her that Mrs Shelley Hughes would be at the mortuary at four o'clock to talk to her. Would she please ring him back if that was *not* going to be convenient and he would re-arrange?

CHAPTER SIX

There was no time to ponder her personal problems. When she returned to the office Jericho was sitting at his desk, his eyes bright with curiosity, hand stroking his grizzled hair in a gesture she knew well.

'Afternoon, Jerry,' she said.

'Mrs Gunn.' He invariably was formal when he was dying to find out some fact or other. He was hopeless at concealing his curiosity. 'How did the post-mortem go?' His voice was casual. It didn't deceive her for a minute.

'I'm not sure.'

His eyes brightened a few more watts. 'But I thought it was an open and shut case.' He was probing.

'I'm beginning to think there's no such thing, Jerry.'

'Really?'

But she was not going to satisfy his inquisitiveness just yet. Jericho Palfreyman was Shropshire born and bred. And while he had the kindest of hearts and was unfailingly understanding with the bereaved he was also an incurable gossip. One of the first to spread rumours. His eyes sparkled all the brighter when he believed there was a juicy bit of scandal behind a case. Martha's greatest fear was that one day he would overstep the mark and leak some precious confidence to someone who would, in turn, relay it to the Press. It would be unforgivable. So she was always extra careful what she told him, even knowing that ultimately he had full access to her records.

'But I thought it was a suicide of a youngster in custody. There's surely no question about that, is there? He was a violent type, wasn't he? Nearly killed that poor lad, he did.'

'I think there's a bit more to 'that poor lad' than we've been led to believe. Maybe we should reserve judgement,' Martha said crisply. Jericho hesitated, shuffled a few papers, patently waiting for her to fill him in but she stepped towards her office door so he substituted any further comment with a, 'Coffee, Mrs Gunn?'

'Thank you.'

She closed the door behind her, manoeuvring between the desk and the chair to stand in front of the bay window and stare out. She often did this when she wanted to think about her role. Mark Sullivan had been uneasy about the PM and so was she. As a doctor herself she knew why they were concerned. Perhaps in an old lady the slightest of knocks made their mark but in a thirteen-year-old bruises didn't just happen and the bruises they had all seen at the post-mortem were the results of blows. The one to Callum's shin, in particular, had been vicious. Almost certainly the result of a kick. The question was from whom? Of course Sullivan's explanation could be the right one. They could all have been the result of innocent encounters – a swerve in the transfer van, banging a shin against the side of the bunk. But she didn't think so. She had learned that each tiny piece of pathology unearthed in a post-mortem was the result of an encounter.

Each had a story to tell. They simply hadn't read the text. Yet.

Jericho appeared with the coffee and she sensed his continuing interest in the case. He lingered as he set it on her desk, fussed about finding a drinks mat. And his interest didn't pall. Right through the rest of the morning he brought her too frequent cups of coffee and at one o'clock a sandwich. A woman called Rose called in daily with a basket of food and Jericho took great delight in selecting Martha's lunchtime menu.

Today it was Coronation chicken on soft, brown bread and a chocolate flapjack. Martha suppressed a smile. Jericho only chose anything with chocolate on the days when *he* decided she was particularly stressed and in for a difficult afternoon.

What was more, he presented them to her on a white, bone china plate with a meaningful grimace of sympathy. Two more signs that he thought she was having a troublesome day. He usually left the sandwiches in their wrapper.

'Jerry,' she said slowly, 'you spoke to Callum's mother?'

'That I did.'

'What did she sound like?'

'Sort of distant,' he said, screwing up his face. 'As though it was all happening to somebody else.'

It was not what Martha had expected. She swivelled her head round to read Jericho's face. 'Not angry?'

Jericho thought for a moment. 'No not angry,' he said slowly. 'Not angry.'

'Perhaps she's been prescribed a sedative.'

Jericho's pale eyes contemplated her. 'She didn't sound groggy,' he offered.

He waited for her next question and when she said nothing

more made a great, bowing ceremony of leaving the room, closing the door noiselessly behind him.

Martha chewed slowly on the sandwich. She was lucky that her office was placed in this huge, Victorian house with its tall, bay windows. It lightened the heaviness of her duties. So much concern with death is bound to sometimes feel like a burden. She crossed the room to the window and stared out, picking out landmarks: the green of the Quarry site of the Shrewsbury Flower Show last month, the spire of St Chad's, the river wrapping around the town. Her office was a little to the south of what had once been known as Scrobbes-byrig (The fortress of Scrob). Shrewsbury is a pretty town, she reflected. She and Martin had felt so fortunate to move here, both of them quickly finding good careers, settling into rural town life. They had been blessed with the twins. All that had seemed fortunate. Too lucky, almost, to last. And so it had proved. Before the twins' third birthday Martin had had the death sentence of his final illness and then for a time the town had seemed isolated, a long way from their families, lonely – even at times hostile.

And now?

She turned back to her desk, to the neat piles of work, the documents waiting to be read, a list of pending telephone calls to be made in Jericho's neat, copperplate handwriting, her laptop. A recent photograph of the twins at Alton Towers, their glee captured for ever as they rode the crest of the waterfall on the Log Flume, they in the front, eyes wide, Sam's crooked teeth, Sukey's blonde hair flying behind her, she and Agnetha, indulgently smiling from the safety of the back seat.

She looked closer at Sam and felt the familiar clutch of her heart. Liverpool seemed *such* a long way away.

She sighed, bent her head and worked steadily for the next hour or so. But it didn't help that a little after two a second text appeared on her phone from Sam, again asking her to ring him that night. What about, she kept thinking, and felt troubled that he'd again added the enquiry about the dog.

Something was wrong, she worried, and pictured Callum Hughes. She had witnessed the cruelty of boys more than once herself, watched, a boy being bullied, outside Sam's school, frightened, yet determined to prove his bravado, the final, humiliating collapse into tears while she had stood by, wanting to intervene yet knowing the boy would be open even more to ridicule if she had.

It had happened in her own school, when she had been eleven years old and two seniors had decided she was laughing at their outlandish, punk hairdos and taken a swipe at her. She considered her son's isolation in such a boy's institution. The mother in her wanted to speak to him now. See him now.

What had caused the bruises on Callum Hughes's face?

Her mobile phone pinged again to remind her that she had a message. There is a frustration in secret codes. Sometimes they are too secret. They hint and give you a clue without being specific. They leave you with a half-knowledge which is sometimes worse than ignorance. The half that you don't know is filled in by the imagination – frequently darker than the truth.

She closed her eyes to shut out the pain.

Until she heard voices outside followed by a soft knock on the door.

She glanced at her watch. It was dead on four o'clock.

Jericho held the door open to a slim woman with red hair. She was young, in her thirties, with vivid blue eyes. She wasn't anything like Martha had imagined.

'Mrs Hughes?'

The woman nodded with more than a hint of aggression in her manner.

'I'm Martha Gunn, the coroner. I thought it was best that we had a talk.'

Shelley Hughes didn't smile. Rather, two lines appeared at either side of her mouth.

'Please. Sit down.'

Martha motioned towards the two leather armchairs which stood in the centre of the room. Sometimes she would sit behind the desk but this was not one of those occasions. This was a time for informality. Shelley Hughes sat in one, crossed her legs and leaned back, her eyes fixed on Martha.

'Would you like a drink?'

'Water.' (No 'please', Martha noted.)

Jericho scuttled off and returned in a minute with a tumbler of water. Then, deliberately, he closed the door behind him.

Martha handed the water to Callum Hughes's mother and sat opposite her. Shelley Hughes's eyes were still on her.

'Do you understand what my role is?'

Shelley Hughes shook her head, sipped her water, set it down on the low table.

'As coroner,' Martha continued, 'my role is to investigate deaths which are reported to me – that is – which appear to be violent or unnatural.'

Something wary entered Shelley Hughes's face.

Martha had met the son. Now she searched the mother's

face for some resemblance. And found none.

Shelley Hughes simply stared back at her, her face marked by a mixture of grief and anger. No not anger. Martha corrected herself. Fury. This woman was furious.

It was difficult not to typecast relatives before you met them – particularly in cases like this. A juvenile offender, a violent crime, a first arrest, a court appearance, a suicide. Martha had visualised a downtrodden woman, one for whom life had been rough and tough. A single parent – like herself. She had pictured prematurely wrinkled skin, badly dyed, dry hair, jeans, a T-shirt.

But Shelley Hughes was nothing like that. She was a slight, pretty woman, neatly and sombrely dressed in a dark suit, low-heeled loafers, a white blouse. She had large, appealing eyes. Her hair was dyed a shining, bright red and was straightened, framing her face. The only detail correct in Martha's mind was the fact that as each minute ticked by Callum Hughes's mother looked older.

Martha had also imagined that Shelley Hughes would be foul-mouthed, venting her fury with expletives. She usually found in such circumstances that the relatives were primarily angry. But Shelley Hughes turned red-rimmed eyes on her expectantly and was silent.

It was Martha who opened up the discussion.

'Tell me about your son,' she said softly.

Shelley Hughes looked surprised. 'You say that like—' Then she was stuck for words.

'Mrs Hughes,' Martha said for the second time. 'My role is not to point fingers but to find out the truth about your son's death. It is a tragedy, both the circumstances which led up to his detention and subsequently to his death. I am appointed by the Crown to ascertain the truth. That is all.'

Shelley Hughes opened her mouth to speak. 'I don't see...'

She didn't understand Martha's methods. Martha felt it would be better, in these circumstances, to ask an open question, invite comment and let her talk.

It was one of Martha's mantras. What greater respect do we owe our dead than to allow their nearest and dearest to speak about them – uninterrupted? Particularly in a sensitive case like this where a youth had been in the charge of another authority. She smiled at Shelley Hughes. Mothers usually enjoy talking about their sons.

But Shelley was suspicious. 'What side of him do you want to see? My son the potential murderer or my son the victim?'

Martha persisted. 'Just tell me about him. Tell me anything which may or may not have a bearing on the assault and subsequently on his death.'

Shelley leaned forward then, her control slipping away from her. Tears filled her eyes up, threatened to overflow and spill down her cheeks. She went pale. 'He was my only boy,' she said, her voice faltering. 'I wasn't married for very long. I only had him. There was just the two of us.'

'Callum's father?'

Shelley's face tightened. 'His father stuck around for all of the first two years of his life,' she said. 'And even then he'd been playing around.'

Her face hardened. She'd known it, had her face rubbed in it. The late nights, the scent of cheap perfume, the excuses, the excuses, the excuses... Sometimes she'd thought he was nothing but excuses. There was no quiet, polite, attentive man who had seemed genuinely to love her. She must have imagined it all. Because once married he had changed, to a man who looked everywhere for female company but within his own four walls. So why had he married her? Perhaps he had loved her once. Who knew? Not her. She had no idea except that she had been deceived and deluded and that there had been no father/son bond.

Shelley wiped her finger across her cheek and looked across at Martha. 'Callum wasn't very well for the first few months,' she said. 'He was sickly. Maybe it was that that put his Dad off him. You know,' she said brightly, 'men like to think of their sons as being strong and…' Her voice tailed off.

Yes, Martha thought, men did like to think of their sons as being strong. She winced. Oh, how Martin would have revelled in Sam's success.

Shelley Hughes continued. 'Callum had asthma. They told me later it was a milk allergy. He screamed a lot.' She blinked and more tears were squeezed out of her eyes.

This was an understatement. Her tiny son had screamed and wheezed his way precariously towards his first birthday. For the first year she and the tiny, sickly infant had virtually lived at the doctor's surgery. Callum had been on permanent antibiotics and syrups, which had, in turn, ruined his teeth, staining them and rotting them simultaneously. Another mark to single him out as someone different, someone separate. Someone not like the others. She turned her attention back to the room.

'I don't know how to say this, Mrs Gunn. It sounds unsympathetic but, Callum, he was sort of born to be picked on.'

'Go on.'

'DreadNought, Roger – the boy that Callum stabbed. He'd been picking on him for a couple of years – ever since Call was about eleven. He'd throw his schoolbag in the road, jostle him, jeer if he got an answer right in class.' Her gaze wavered towards the window. 'It just went on and on. He never stopped. I didn't know what to do to help. If I'd have said something it would have made everything worse.'

'Was there no one you could speak to?'

Shelley shook her head. 'I did say something to one of the teachers but he wanted to make it official and I...I was so afraid of making things worse. DreadNought was a big, popular boy.'

'I understand,' Martha said. 'Go on.'

'DreadNought.' She must have picked up something in Martha's gaze. 'What is it?'

'I'm afraid Roger Gough is – quite poorly,' Martha said.

Shelley stared back at her uncomprehending. 'What do you mean?'

'It seems he's picked up an infection in the hospital. They're trying to make his lung re-inflate but he's in Intensive Care and they're worried about him.'

The two women stared at each other. Shelley spoke first, her face white and shocked. 'If Call...' She swallowed, 'if Call had lived are you saying he might be up for murder? Is it that bad?'

'I'm not in charge of Roger Gough's care,' Martha said. 'But I do know it was a serious injury. And with infection...' She let the sentence hang. Incomplete – unsatisfactory – like the entire case. Pointless and futile. All because a boy had picked on another boy and the victim had suddenly turned tables to become villain. She felt a sudden hot wash of anger. Why had nothing been done?

Shelley simply stared at her.

'I'm not investigating the assault on Roger Gough,' Martha said, 'but your son's death. Why did he assault Roger Gough on that particular day? Was there anything special about it?'

Shelley Hughes shook her head. 'It was always going to build up to something. Callum was getting to the point when he'd had enough. He was like a volcano ready to blow. I could sense it. He'd go out of the door, his face red and angry and take these clomping big steps. I knew one day he wouldn't be able to stop himself. He'd just lash out – whatever the consequences. And I think it just happened to be that day. Chance.'

'Did you know he'd bought a knife?'

Shelley shook her head. 'I'd have stopped him.'

'So you thought it would be a fight?'

Shelley nodded, her hair swinging.

Martha drew in a deep breath. 'Let's go through what happened on Tuesday night, shall we?'

'The police came and told me Call had been involved in something. I thought at first he'd been beaten up by DreadNought.'

'So you went to the police station?'

'They let me take him in some clothes – his computer games, iPod.'

'How did he seem?'

'Like he was in a dream. Like he couldn't believe what he'd just done.'

'And he'd bought the knife quite a while before – and sharpened it.'

'I know, I know.' Now it was Shelley who was agitated – rising up out of her chair. 'I know – but I don't think until he stuck it in DreadNought that he thought he'd use it.'

'So you think he was shocked?'

Shelley nodded her head vigorously. 'Yeah. It was just like that. He couldn't believe what he'd done.'

'Right.'

Martha allowed the words to sink in for a while before pursuing her enquiry. 'So he spent the night at the police station?'

'Yes.'

'And I take it you were at the magistrates' court on Wednesday morning?'

'I wouldn't have missed it. I had to be there for him. He needed someone. It was the last time I saw him. Until...'

Martha could fill in. She tried to move Shelley Hughes on. 'How was he after his first night in custody?'

'He was still in a sort of dream,' Shelley said. 'Dazed. I don't think it had hit him.'

'Did you worry about how he would respond when it did?'

The big eyes stared back at her, almost frozen. Then Shelley nodded again. 'He asked me how DreadNought was. I understood then that he was going to be OK. He was upset that people were outside the court calling him names and the newspaper people took some pictures. I think he worried he'd always be labelled as this sort of psycho.'

'Mrs Hughes,' Martha said. 'I want you to think carefully about this before you answer. Had Callum ever mentioned suicide to you? Had he ever tried before? Had you ever seen him experiment with ropes – a noose?'

Shelley seemed to pause, as though suspended in time. Then slowly she shook her head. 'Never before this,' she said. 'But yesterday, when I was talking to him after he'd been in the court, when they told him he was going to Stoke Heath, he said, 'I might as well be dead.' She lifted her big eyes to look straight at Martha. 'I worried then but I thought they'd keep an eye on him.'

To Martha it seemed final. Callum had said he might as well be dead and that night he had carried out his statement. It seemed to clinch things. She allowed Shelley Hughes some moments of silence to reach the same conclusion herself. And she did.

'He couldn't see his way to doing a stretch. Not years. It would have finished him. And he'd have been on remand for months. The police told him that. Cases take ages to come to court. Call wasn't strong, you see, Mrs Gunn. He knew he'd be different from the other boys in there. He knew they'd pick on him, that every day would be like a school day with no break. No weekends when he could stay in with me and no Mum either. We were close. At least he had me to come home to. Much good I did him,' she finished bitterly, her mouth tightening into a thin, straight line.

The effort of saying this seemed to finish her. She covered her face with her hands and openly wept, great racking sobs. 'He was all I had,' she said. 'I got nothing now.'

It was a bleak statement.

Martha sat by, motionless. Words of so-called comfort would have seemed an insult.

When Shelley finally took her hands away and stopped crying, she handed her the box of tissues. As she had done to countless other relatives she explained the formality of the inquest system and said that Jericho would inform her when it was to be. Shelley stood up. Martha spoke. 'If at any time you want to contact me Jericho will give you our telephone number. The inquest allows you the opportunity to speak about your son. You might feel you want someone to speak up for Callum. His case will not now be tried in a court of law but you may feel you want, in some way, to say something positive about him. Is there anyone?'

Shelley Hughes didn't even pause. 'One of his teachers,' she said. 'His History teacher, Mr Farthing. He had a good opinion of my lad. He saw the good in him. I'll contact him.'

Once again Martha extended her condolences and promised to keep in touch and Shelley Hughes left.

Martha sat alone.

Until Jericho bustled back in with a mug of steaming coffee.

Alex Randall had asked Police Constable Gethin Roberts to drive him out to Stoke Heath but even though the traffic was light and Roberts a competent driver he still sat, tensely, in the car, his mind disturbed by something intangible. A cold, uneasy feeling that something was wrong. His mind kept returning to the picture of the boy: thin, frightened, hunched over the table – and the lad's mother: hostile, accusatory, her eyes begging him to do something. He didn't relish meeting her again. He knew, however illogical it might be, that she must blame him for her son's death and in a way this was the pig-end of a death in custody. The police were to some extent responsible. They were the failed protectors. On instinct he used the car phone to get Doctor Porter's telephone number. Callum's untimely death had robbed him of the chance to explain, maybe even to exonerate his actions. He connected with the doctor and asked him if he remembered having a phone call from Shelley Hughes, asking him about fractured ribs.

It was a long shot. Which didn't pay off. The doctor was friendly.

'But to be honest, Inspector Randall, if Mrs Hughes had asked a general question I probably wouldn't remember the telephone call and certainly wouldn't have logged it on. I would have asked her if she had any specific concerns and left it at that.'

'Thanks.' Alex disconnected.

Roberts parked the car neatly outside the high walls in one of the bays and they approached the huge doors, big enough for the security vans to drive right through. Alex Randall waited impatiently while the formalities were observed for entry to the institution. The desk officer was initially unfriendly, defensive. He knew that they were dreading this investigation. That the finger must ultimately point towards them for their failure.

Alex pushed such sensitivities out of his mind. First of all he asked to speak, alone, to Tyrone Smith.

It took them a few valuable minutes to locate Tyrone Smith and escort him down to the interview room. Smith was an overweight, lumbering guy, who had something dangerous which clung to the air around him. From the quick, jerky movements to the wild look held in the dark eyes he was a person to keep your eye on, a physical presence you could not help but be aware of, the sort of person you watched out of the corner of your eye and didn't drop your guard with. He had big hands, which he quickly bunched into fists, as Randall questioned him. Once or twice he shifted in his chair and Randall immediately tensed up.

He was the sort to enjoy inflicting pain.

Randall surveyed him.

Tyrone sniffed and watched him like an animal, tensing itself to pounce, snarling and clawing into its prey.

Randall introduced himself. 'I'm Detective Inspector Randall,' he said. 'I'm the senior officer investigating Callum Hughes's death. I want you to tell me anything that you can.'

Smith said nothing.

'Then just tell me about last night,' he began.

'I had my tea,' Smith said. His voice was lardy and slow, his accent rural Shropshire, with a distinct burr.

'At what time?'

'I don't know. Same time as normal. Five. Six. Sumatt like that. We're allowed to watch a bit of TV till ten. I was back in my cell when the screws come up with this fellah.'

'Tell me about the fellah.'

Smith considered. 'He looked dead scared,' he said, waving bravado with his hands.

'I could tell he was a first-timer. A saddo. A mother-wanter.'

Alex Randall watched Smith through half-closed eyes. He had thought that years in the police would have inured him to characters like this and yet, he could feel dislike seeping through his skin.

'Go on.'

'He was skinny and scared. The screws made some crack about him and left him with me.'

'Did you speak to him?'

'Hardly. He kept trying to offer me fags and chocolate and things like he could bribe me to like him. Actually I didn't want nothin' to do with him. I could tell he was bad news.'

'What do you mean 'bad news'?'

'Unstable like.'

'Are you saying you thought he was likely to hang himself?'

Tyrone Smith puffed his chest out like a bird of paradise. 'No. 'Course not. If I'd have thought that I'd have told the screws – wouldn't I?'

Almost intelligently he waited for Randall's reply. 'I suppose you would have done, Smith.'

Tyrone looked a touch disappointed at the policeman's response. 'No, what I meant were, he was in for violent attack.'

Like you, Alex thought.

'Did you threaten him?'

Slowly Smith shook his head.

'Verbally or physically?'

Again that slow, definite shake of the head.

'Think carefully, Smith.' Alex Randall leaned forward to eyeball him. 'He had some injuries.'

'Well they weren't nothin' to do with me.'

He would say that, wouldn't he?

'Did anyone else come into the cell?'

'Screws a couple of times. Just to check on my new little brother – as it were.'

'Inside or outside the cell?'

Smith eyed Randall curiously. 'What're you askin' me for? Ask them. They was there.' He stopped speaking, held his breath. 'Look. It weren't my fault he topped himself.'

'What do you remember of his suicide?'

'I slept right through it, Mr Policeman. Don't remember a thing.'

'Are you expecting me to believe that?'

'I don't care whether you believe it or not. You can't prove otherwise.'

Alex Randall felt a pricking of his mind. He watched Smith's greasy face and saw a small, evasive fluttering of his eyes. Oh – there was something here. He'd rattled him. He kept his gaze on Smith, trying to sense what exactly Smith had witnessed but Smith's face had sunk back into a bland expression. The flicker of fear had disappeared.

'So then what?'

'You know what. I woke up this mornin' and he was hangin' there. Dead as a dodo with great, starin' eyes.' Smith frowned. 'Horrible they were. I was traumatised. I started bangin' on my cell door. And then the two screws came.'

'Which two?'

'The two who'd been on all night,' Smith said, as though explaining to a child. 'The old one, Pembroke, and his new rookie, the woman. The little one with the big arse.'

'And what did they do?'

'What do you think? Cursed and swore, touched him and pressed the emergency bell. There was panic, I can tell you. Everyone scuttlin' around, swearin' and cursin'. They got me out of my cell and put me in a holdin' bay. That's all I know. That's it. Sum total.'

He tried to stare innocently at Randall. But Smith had very pale, blue eyes enveloped in podgy eyelids. Randall put his face close to Smith's. 'Are you trying to tell me that you heard nothing?'

'Not a thing.'

'You didn't hear your cellmate get out of bed?'

Smith shook his head.

'Or remove the flex from the back of the computer?'

Again Smith shook his head, his eyes firmly locked into the policeman's. He was a good liar.

'You didn't hear him loop it around the bed – or fall?'

Randall could anticipate what Smith's next response would be.

Correct.

'You didn't hear him die? Any sound at all?'

'No, Sir.' Smith stared right past him and for the briefest of moments Randall almost wondered if Smith had any feelings. Guilt? Pity?

It would have been nice.

Randall gave a deep sigh and wondered exactly what had happened because he didn't believe this version.

'Did you kick him? On the leg?'

'No. As if. Mind you...'

Randall could guess what would come next.

'...Now I think about it he did bang himself against the desk. Quite hard.'

Correct. Except.

'The injury was more consistent with a kick than a bang against a flat surface. The pathologist could tell by the pattern of bruising.'

'Clever – ain't they?'

Slowly Randall nodded.

'You can go, Smith. But I may want to talk to you again.' He couldn't resist the jibe, 'I'll know where to find you.'

It provoked a pugnacious squaring of the jaw but nothing else.

So now Randall merely had to concentrate on the two prison officers who had been kept in the prison but allowed to sleep for the morning. Until the enquiry was complete they would be suspended from duty.

He interviewed Walton Pembroke first.

The senior prison officer sauntered in with an arrogant confidence, sat down without being asked and crossed his legs.

Randall performed the introductions again.

'How long have you been in the prison service?'

'Thirty years. I go next year. On a full pension.' Pembroke sounded well satisfied with his life.

Randall managed a sympathy-smile. 'That must be something to look forward to.'

Walton Pembroke dipped his head in an acknowledgment. 'After a lifetime here it is. I can tell you.'

'Have you always worked here?'

'Nope. Worked at Winson Green, Shrewsbury. Even a stretch at Gartree. Didn't like it there though.'

'You must have met some right villains.'

Pembroke gave a grimace of a smile. 'Nah,' he said, attempting a joke. 'They're all innocent. Lovely people really.'

Randall tried to laugh too but the humour was thin. The truth was that appeals from prison, long after they'd been sentenced, still sent shivers up his spine. It meant revising old cases instead of solving new. Quite apart from the aspersions it cast on the police force, false statements, erroneous evidence. It didn't do the justice system any good. Dragging officers out of retirement. Half-remembered facts, memories playing tricks. 'Is this your writing?'

Who knew? Some of the officers, witnesses, would have died anyway. Reopening cases, in Randall's opinion, always meant trouble.

'Look, Mr Pembroke' he said, his face deliberately straight. 'We're on the same side, you and I. Let's work together. You know this is a serious case. I want you to tell me, right from the start, the encounter you had with young Callum Hughes.'

The approach stopped Pembroke short. He narrowed his eyes as he looked back at Randall. Randall could hear his brain cranking into action to wonder whether to take the policeman at face value – or not.

'Group 4 brought him to us at nine,' he said. 'By the time we'd checked him and clerked in all his belongings it was half past. It was ten by the time we took him to his cell.'

Randall interrupted. 'Whose choice was it to put him in with Tyrone Smith?'

For the first time Walton Pembroke looked uncomfortable. 'I don't know,' he said. 'I don't rightly remember. It was probably decided by the day shift.'

Randall leaned in closer. 'And what did you think when you knew a vulnerable young lad like Hughes was to be locked up with a thug for ten hours?'

Pembroke swallowed and Randall knew, he just knew that the prison officers had derived some 'innocent fun' out of it.

Part of the job. Got to have a laugh at work – haven't you?

'They're all young thugs,' he said finally. 'He wasn't going to share a cell with Christopher Robin and Pooh Bear.' It was the best he could come up with.

'How many suicides have you had in Stoke Heath since you've been here?'

Pembroke shook his head. 'None.'

'And at the other places where you have worked?'

'One or two,' Pembroke said. 'You can't stop people killing their selves. If they want to do it they'll do it.'

Randall kept his face impassive.

'Then what?'

'We did our rounds.'

Again Randall sensed evasion. Little more than a change in the temperature of the room, a slight quickening of Pembroke's breathing, a rubbing together of sweating palms. 'At what time?'

'We go round a couple of times early on in the night – eleven-ish, twelve-ish.'

'Into the cells?'

'Sometimes.'

Again Randall studied the prison officer for a few long moments. 'Did you go into cell 101?'

Pembroke nodded.

'Both times?'

Again Pembroke nodded.

'Is this usual?'

Pembroke shifted uncomfortably. 'It depends.'

'On what?'

'Whether they're awake or asleep.'

Randall squared his face against the other's. 'And in this case?'

Junior officers would have recognised the deceptive softening of the tone.

'Smith was out for the count.' Pembroke licked his lips.

'And Hughes,' Randall queried, still softly, asking himself the question, why was he having to work so hard, teasing every tiny detail out of a senior officer?

'Hughes was upset,' Pembroke said. 'He was crying the first time. We went in and he tried to jip it out of the cell. We let him out along the corridor. Just for a walk. They suffer like that a bit...' Randall sensed the prison officer was back on home ground. Home and dry. Safe and sound.

'First night and all that. Their stretch seems as if it'll go on forever. They don't think they'll ever be out. No dates for hearings. Miss their mothers. Bound to get a bit upset.'

'Understand young lads, do you?'

Pembroke flushed. 'I don't get what you're saying.'

'You're working in a Young Offenders'.' Randall spoke smoothly. 'I just thought you might have some special understanding with them. That's all.'

'Not in any sort of personal way,' Pembroke said defensively, almost truculently. 'But I've a couple of sons of my own. One working in Shrewsbury prison. I can get along with them most times. I didn't take this job to get close to vulnerable young lads if that's what you're implying.'

'Right. So – did you need to restrain young Hughes?'

Pembroke managed a laugh. 'Oh no. He was one of your timid sorts. Once we'd let him have a turn around the corridor he was fine to go back in.'

'And the second time?'

'Fast asleep. Like Smith. Sleeping like a baby.'

'I should just tell you that there were some bruises on his face, his leg.'

'Nothin' to do with any of us, Inspector Randall.'

'The pathologist asked if the body was slumped against the bed or free swinging. How long was the computer cord?'

Pembroke hesitated. Then he said 'Tight. There was no room for movement.'

'Thank you.' Randall had the impression that Walton Pembroke had been unsure how to answer this question.

Interesting.

'OK. You're free to go, Pembroke.' He waited until he had reached the door. 'If you do think of anything you'd like to add to your statement you know where I can be reached.'

Randall watched him go with a feeling close to unhappiness. He didn't quite trust Walton Pembroke. There was something too slick about the man. He was too restless to speak to the woman officer. Before he moved on he decided he would take another peep at cell 101.

The corridors looked long and, in his current frame of mind, menacing with doors every few feet. The cells must be tiny. He looked up and met the unblinking eye of the video watching him.

He'd take the tapes back to the station and get a couple of sharp-eyed rookies to drink coffee and watch them just in case there was anything of interest, any clue. They could freeze-frame young Callum Hughes's last moments. He looked up again at the CCTV. It was trained practically outside Callum's cell. That walk along the corridor. He ducked underneath the police tape and peered round the door. It was a small room, floor space maximised by bunks up against the wall. Thank God the habit of slopping out had stopped. The toilets were cleaned by the inmates every morning. The cell smelt primarily of bleach. The window was ajar, a faint breeze blowing the scent through.

For a tiny room a lot had been packed in. A computer, two cupboards, plenty of posters, toilet and sink, bars across the windows.

Randall looked out on the courtyard, then, on impulse, he crossed to the door and banged it shut. Yes, if he was a young lad of thirteen or so, in for the first night of what would almost certainly be a long stretch, he too would feel claustrophobic.

CHAPTER SEVEN

It was with a feeling of relief that he walked away from the cell and returned to the interview room.

Stevie Matthews was sitting outside, waiting for him, her hands tucked underneath her legs, gulping for air.

'The little one with the big arse.'

He smiled. The regulation trousers did nothing for her, white blouse tucked in giving her the look of a sack of spuds tied around the middle. She was pale with thin dark hair which straggled to her shoulders and anxious, tired eyes. He knew she had not slept in her free morning. However tired she had been she had not relaxed.

'Sit down,' he invited, after introducing himself.

Instantly he could tell the difference between her and Walton Pembroke. Pembroke had been so sure of himself, sure of his job and position too whereas she was a nervous wreck. Randall wondered. Was it simply the senior officer's years on the job plus the fat carrot of a good pension or some confidence inbuilt?

Stevie was new, nervous, uncertain what to say. And frightened.

Of what?

That she'd lose her job?

He watched her sit down and wondered how on earth she would survive her years as a 'screw'. She simply didn't look tough enough.

He tried to put her at her ease with a smile and a preamble. 'Stevie,' he said. 'I suppose it's short for...?'

'Stephanie.' She had a squeaky, high-pitched voice.

'But you prefer Stevie.'

She nodded and he knew that the simple little ruse had succeeded. She was just starting to unwind.

'How long have you worked here for, Stevie?'

'A month.'

'First stretch of nights?'

She nodded again.

'So this is pretty much a nightmare for you.'

'Terrible.'

'Tell me about your encounter with young Hughes. What did you think of him?'

She swallowed with a noisy gulp. 'He seemed quiet. Not a problem. Some of them...' She was warming to her subject, 'they swagger. They're so cocky and full of themselves – almost as if they were proud to be here. Loads of them boast they'll get off, that they've got influence, a clever lawyer, stuff like that. Hughes didn't hardly say anything.'

'Can you remember who took the decision to put him in with Tyrone Smith?'

'No. I don't have much to do with decisions like that. I only knew he was to go in there. I think Walton told me.'

'And what did you think of that?'

She regarded him silently and he knew the true answer was

nothing. She had not thought about it. It told him something about her.

She was unimaginative.

A lack of imagination can be very useful to the police. Unimaginative people make poor, uninspired liars – unless fed by others. They tend to tell the truth. Her very dullness encouraged him.

'You put Callum in his cell then saw him again at around eleven?'

Stevie nodded and flicked a string of hair away from her face. 'We always go and see the new ones, make sure they're settling in. Some get really scared, you see. Mr Pembroke...'

Something stopped her short. She pressed her lips together, Randall noted but made no comment. He suspected misguided loyalty to her senior colleague and probed innocently. 'I expect Mr Pembroke has been a great help to you – being experienced in the prison service?'

Prison Officer Matthews nodded her head vigorously. 'Yeah. He's been great. Really helpful. It's made my first weeks here a lot more pleasant.'

Randall could well imagine it. The wide-eyed innocence of Matthews would have fattened Pembroke's ego up nicely. 'Pleasant,' he queried innocently. 'In what way?'

'He stopped me being made a fool of, taught me how to suss them out.'

Randall raised his eyebrows.

'He knows all the tricks.'

Randall licked his lips. 'All the tricks?'

'Yeah. Like they say they get asthma or pretend they've got stomach-ache or something like that. Just for attention. You know? To get out of their cells.' Her limpid, pale eyes watched him.

'And that's what you did, of course, with young Callum Hughes. Took him out of his cell. Why?'

'He was in a bit of a bad way. Lying there, shaking on his bed, all scrunched into the corner. He was in a right state so we let him have a turn along the corridor.'

She was not looking at him, Randall noted, but at a fixed point on the wall, slightly to his right side, a little over his shoulder. Again he made no comment but squirreled the fact away. He suspected that the lessons Walton Pembroke had taught his new young colleague had been connected with domination and intimidation rather than interpersonal skills.

'Did he say anything when you walked him up the corridor? Anything that made you suspect that he was suicidal?'

Stevie Matthews looked upset. 'No. Nothing,' she protested. 'We'd have put him on suicide watch if we'd had any idea.'

But she was still fixing on that point on the wall so he pushed forward. 'I take it that when you allowed Callum out of his cell you locked the door behind you?'

'Oh, yes. It's standard practice.'

There is something depressing about employees who trot out the company line a little too tritely, Randall reflected. They would always quote 'company practice'. Such a useful phrase to hide behind.

'And what was Tyrone Smith doing when you took Callum out of the cell?'

For the first time since she had entered Stevie Matthews smiled and relaxed. She was surer of this ground. 'Asleep,' she giggled. 'Like a baby. Snoring his big fat head off.'

'And was Callum happy to return to his cell?'

The prison officer nodded.

'We had a little chat with him,' she said. 'We explained the rules, how he could make his life easier if he fell in with us. He was happy enough then. A bit more settled. We never guessed.' Her eyes changed shape. They were round with the horror. The vision of Callum Hughes, slumped against the bed was obviously what had upset her.

Randall waited before his next question. So often it is silence which encourages people to talk rather than banter.

'And the second time?' he prompted.

'Callum was asleep too,' she said quickly.

'Did you go inside the cell?'

Oddly enough Stevie Matthews seemed unsure how to answer the question. She looked confused.

At such a simple question?

Randall repeated it.

'Did you go inside the cell?'

Matthews jerked and nodded as though she'd found her lines. 'We thought we'd better just check on him.'

'Why?'

'He'd seemed so upset earlier. And it was his first night in custody.'

'Was Tyrone Smith still asleep on your *second* visit?'

Stevie Matthews smiled. 'He was. Snorin' like an express train.'

'I'm sorry to ask you again but on your second visit – at

about twelve – Callum was asleep and in good health.'

'Yeah – as far as I know. I mean...' She bit her lip. 'I didn't touch him or anything.'

'Miss Matthews. I want you to think carefully. Is it possible Callum was faking being asleep?'

'I don't know.'

'Because if he wasn't he must have woken up and then decided to...' There was no need to finish the sentence.

He moved on. 'So then what?'

'The alarm went off about six-thirty. There was panic stations. Me and Walton went to cell 101. Tyrone Smith was hammering on the door, screaming.' Her face crumpled. She was losing control. 'We unlocked the door and there was Callum, slumped against the bed, the wire round his neck.' Her face was distorted with the horror. Her eyes bulged. 'I've never seen anything like it in my life.' She covered her mouth with her hand. 'It was horrible. I couldn't believe it.' Her face held something bleak. Something approaching despair.

'Nearly finished,' he said heartily. 'Just one other area. When Doctor Sullivan did the post-mortem Callum was found to have some minor injuries. Bruising on his face, a blow to his chest and quite marked bruising on his right shin. Do you have any idea how he came by any of these injuries?'

She shook her head.

'Did he at any time resist arrest?'

Again she shook her head, her eyes fixing on his face. Beseeching him – begging him to believe her? Or to simply bring the interview to a close?

'You never had to restrain him?'

Another jerky shake of the head.

He nodded. 'When you entered the cell and found him hanging did you try to resuscitate him?'

'Walton said it was pointless. He was cold.'

'And the bedding?'

She frowned. She couldn't see the point of this question. 'All loose,' she said curtly. 'Hanging down. I didn't take a lot of notice.'

'And Tyrone Smith?'

'He looked sort of shocked. When we unlocked the door he was backed against the window. He was holding his hands up. 'I never done nothing,' he was saying over and over again. 'I didn't do nothin'. It weren't me'.'

Randall could well imagine it. Smith would be like that, he thought.

'Is there anything else you want to add?'

Stevie Matthews shook her head again.

'OK,' he said. 'You're free to go.'

She bolted, like a child out of school. When she had gone Alex Randall sat for a while, pondering. He'd learnt nothing by coming here today. He could have guessed most of it.

Or could he?

He called in at the front desk for the CCTV tapes and left Stoke Heath with a feeling of relief. It might be his job to put these youngsters behind bars but the place depressed him.

He took the tapes back to the station and handed them over to a couple of duty officers. They could spend the evening being paid for watching telly. It was his usual quip but they grinned obediently. He glanced at his watch. It was a quarter past eight and he felt the usual reluctance to going home. Home was trouble. Home was conflict. He sat in his office, his face buried in his hands.

At nine he could put it off no longer. He must go to what passed as a home.

Martha finally got through to Sam at nine-thirty and instantly knew that he was not alone. She could hear the evasion, the embarrassment in his voice, the hesitation when she asked her question. Perhaps now he rarely was alone but always with someone. 'Is everything all right, Sam?'

'Yeah, of course.'

But she knew it wasn't. Something was wrong. It might be nothing – a minor problem – a missed kick, a clumsy pass. Or something else. And now, to herself, she acknowledged that she was worried Sam would be bullied, picked on and would retaliate. It wasn't that there was some similarity between Callum Hughes and Sam Gunn but that there are some common points between *all* boys of thirteen years old. They are all chrysalis men, trying to prove themselves.

'We thought we'd come up over the weekend, Sam?' She left the question hovering and again was aware of another presence physically nearer to her son than hers.

'Is that OK?'

She sensed a theatrical shrug. 'If you like. We've got a friendly against another Junior Premiership.'

'What time?'

'Kick-off five on Saturday.'

She knew that he would be unable to concentrate before a match and afterwards she didn't want to rob him of the camaraderie of either a triumphant or defeated football team. 'What about Sunday then?'

'If you like.'

She spent the rest of the evening seething with frustration and self-doubt. Maybe it had been the wrong decision to let him go. He was too young. To channel him into sport had been the wrong decision. And yet it had been what he had wanted.

At thirteen years old?

Overridingly, she worried what was happening up there?

Randall had given the video tapes to two young officers, Detective Constables Harris and Jenkins who spent the evening munching crisps, drinking coke and watching telly. Only the videotapes were boring. Hours of nothing which they fast-forwarded, slowing down when the prison officers did their rounds.

It took them over an hour to find anything of interest. Then they both sat up.

In grainy black and white they watched the shorter prison officer turn the key to what must be Hughes and Smith's cell. Straightaway Callum pushed forward. They saw Pembroke push him back with an elbow but Hughes came forward again. He was obviously saying something, protesting, pleading. And it seemed to work. Stevie Matthews actually pulled Hughes, locking the door behind him. Next they saw him being frogmarched between the two prison officers. They could see all but hear no noise. Yet they could sense the terror of the lad. He was wild, bumping along the narrow walkway. His shoulders were hunched. At one point he almost slumped against the female prison officer. Then he seemed to try and make a break. The camera was poorly angled so they didn't see the outcome but seconds later he was being manhandled back into the cell with a shove.

Then there was a return to the hours of long, empty corridors.

'I bet that broke up the monotony of the night,' DC Harris remarked. The other swigged from the coke can. 'And we think *our* job's boring.' He slammed the can back on the table and fast-forwarded.

'This must be when they went in for the second time.'

This time there was no sighting of Hughes. The two prison officers went into the cell, stayed there for a while and then emerged, Walton Pembroke with his arm draped loosely across Stevie Matthews' shoulders. They both glanced up straight into the camera before vanishing from sight.

The third sighting of the pair was completely different. This time they were running, unaware of the video eye or anything but a clumsy haste to enter the cell. Stevie Matthews had trouble inserting the key in the lock. She was fumbling. Panicking. They ran in and must have pressed the emergency button again because officers seemed to appear from everywhere.

The two officers marked the places on the tapes and left them on Randall's desk.

Something about the Callum Hughes case stayed with Martha. The first thing she thought about when she awoke the next morning was the boy's mother, determined, brave. Admirable really. She sat up in bed, hugging her knees and listening to the awful silence. Without Sam the house was too quiet. She wondered how Shelley Hughes was coping with the silence? At least *she* had Sukey and Agnetha. Shelley Hughes had no one. Simply an empty house surrounded by hostile neighbours.

She tried to will her thoughts on. It is never a good idea to become too involved in a case. A coroner must, inevitably, move from death to death, like a spectre in a graveyard, dealing with one only to move straightaway to another tragedy, another loss. She knew this. It was part of the job. And yet this one small, tragic case was holding her fast. It was easy to speculate why. Her own son, the same age as Callum Hughes, had also recently left home. Two mothers. And – surely – there were more. War, boarding school, broken homes where the offspring stayed with the father. There were plenty of incidences where mothers and sons were separated.

There was a soft knock at the door. Sukey entered, gingerly carrying a mug. 'Agnetha boiled up the kettle,' she said. 'I thought you might like a coffee.'

Martha felt a rush of pride and affection for her daughter, leggy, Nordic blonde. 'Thanks,' she said and felt an overwhelming instinct to pat the bed and invite her to share confidences. 'I thought we'd go and see Sam on Sunday,' she said.

Sukey wrinkled her nose up. 'Not sit through a game?'

'No. He's playing on Saturday.'

'Great.' Sukey continued to look unexcited. 'So he'll either be really full of himself or down in the dumps because he's fluffed a goal.'

'Come on, Sukes,' Martha cajoled. 'It's his life. It's important to him.'

Sukey's eyes sparkled. 'All right then,' she said, 'if we must. I think Agnetha wants to go to London anyway. Her boyfriend's over for a holiday.'

'Then he must come here for a few days.'

'He might not want to.'

'Well – we can at least ask him.'

'OK.' Sukey climbed off the bed. 'I'll suggest it to her.'

'It would be better coming from me.'

Behind the White House were some woods: largely pine and Spruce trees which dropped their needles onto a soft path. Once Sukey had departed for school with Agnetha driving her Martha walked the familiar trail, Bobby bounding ahead of her, returning every few minutes to lick her hand and reassure himself that he was still the number one dog in her life. An early autumnal mist gave the ground an insubstantial appearance, looking as though the trees were planted not in the ground but in a soft swathe of cotton wool. The dampness of autumn had already crept in, giving a chill to the morning. She was glad to return to the warmth of the house and a shower.

She glanced along her wardrobe. As soon as the autumn fashions reached the shops she always planned her outfits for the next few months. Her practice was to lay all her garments on the bed, choose the ones she still enjoyed wearing, throw away the mistakes and clothes which she no longer wore and then plan a few extra outfits for the autumn and winter. One of her newest purchases had been a plum-coloured suit with an A-line skirt in a soft wool. She had loved the feel of it and bought it for just such a day as today. Cold, bright and with no inquests. Underneath the jacket she wore an ivory T-shirt.

She stood back and felt pleased with the result. Next she swiped her face with make-up and brushed her hair. As usual it was ready for a cut. She wrinkled her nose into the mirror. She was sure that her hair grew faster than other people's. Today, she vowed, she would make an appointment and run the gauntlet of her hairdresser Vernon Grubb's wrath. Too thick. Too unruly. Too wild. She did her best, sprayed on a product guaranteed to 'tame the wildest hair' as well as giving it an 'enviable gloss'. She sighed. How she wished she could believe the claims made by the manufacturers of expensive beauty products. *Ten years younger, clear, youthful skin, a glow to shed years...*What woman over thirty wouldn't be tempted? The shampoo hadn't lived up to its promise.

She was even more glad she had worn her new suit when, a little after eleven, Jericho rang her desk phone.

'Detective Inspector Randall wants to know if you've got a minute,' he said flatly. Jericho did not approve of anybody interrupting her work except him.

'Put him through, Jerry,' she said.

'Martha.' Alex's voice sounded friendly. Strong, vital – very alive. 'I don't know whether you'd be interested but we've got the footage of the CCTV video at the prison. I suppose it shows something of the last hours of Callum's life. I thought you might see something there that explained his suicide.' He paused. 'I don't suppose you'd be interested?'

He knew her too well. He had only rung her because he'd known she would be intrigued.

She accepted.

'Look – why don't I get some sandwiches in and we can watch it together in the station?'

She agreed and ran the gauntlet of Jericho's further disapproval by telling him she was out for lunch.

She drove to Monkmoor station and found Alex in his office. Office sounds grand but in reality it was a busy area shared with a few of his colleagues. She sat at his scratched old desk in an uncomfortable chair. But the bottles of water and Greek salad sandwiches looked appetising.

He flicked the blinds down and they sat down to watch.

Like the other officers Martha found the grainy shots disappointing as the two officers stalked the cells, throwing open doors. And then...

Martha sat up. There he was. Much as she had imagined him. In the flesh and alive but with only a few short hours to go. Thin-shouldered, short dark hair, the boy she had only seen in death. She watched him burst out of his cell and the officer catching him. The camera had captured him walking towards it, the two prison officers either side while the boy between them staggered. Martha peered closer. It looked as though Callum was gasping for air. She remembered his mother telling her the boy was asthmatic. There was nothing more guaranteed to provoke an asthma attack than a night in the cells with Tyrone Smith. But at least they were allowing him to take a walk. The boy's gait was jerky. His shoulders heaved. It was impossible to tell – the picture was so bad. But it looked now as though he was crying. Sobbing. Martha could almost hear him. She stopped eating her sandwich. Callum Hughes looked wretched. She offered up a silent prayer.

Please – don't let Sam be so unhappy.

She pushed her attention back to the video. They were

walking him back to the cell. And he didn't want to go. They were supporting him. One either side. They practically had to throw him back in.

Martha felt unbearably moved by it.

'Poor boy,' she said.

Randall pressed the stop switch. 'The rest of the tape only shows the two officers entering the cell and leaving it and then the mayhem after the alarm was raised.

Martha stood up and thanked Randall. He looked curiously at her. 'So does it explain his death?'

She turned her gaze to him. 'Oh yes,' she said. 'I think it does. Is there anything else?'

'Not that it throws any real light on things,' he said. 'Only that Gavin Morrison – Tyrone Smith's ex-cell mate said that, interestingly, Smith set out certain rules when they first shared a cell together. No snoring, lights out when he said, he had to be first to the bog in the morning. Things like that. As long as he kept to the rules he was OK. But once he must have let out a snort and he woke up to feel Smith's fingers clamped around his throat.'

'Nice.'

'He also confirmed that Smith was an insomniac and would kill for sleeping tablets.'

'Doesn't surprise me,' she said.

She drove back to her office and Jericho handed her a pile of papers. She groaned when she saw what their subject was. So she spent the afternoon going through recent deaths from MRSA both in the community and in the local hospital. Three death certificates sat on her desk with the infamous superbug cited as a contributory cause. One from the community and the other two in the hospital. She knew that the media would attempt to make a story out of it and felt defeated. It was pointless to say that these were already-sick people who had lost the ability to mobilise their immune systems. She stared out over the town. Sometimes she felt like its shepherd. But like a good shepherd sometimes you have to lead your flock to the place of the skull. It might be an unpalatable fact but we are not immortal. No health service, no doctor, no Florence Nightingale of a nurse can make us so.

She did not want to start pointing fingers at her inquests. And yet it was incumbent on her to do so. It was expected of her. She read through the medical facts, checking her mobile phone every few minutes. But from Sam there was nothing.

And that, in a way, was harder.

CHAPTER EIGHT

Martha studied the man in front of her. Slim, round-shouldered, small rimless glasses, a scruffy sports jacket over baggy trousers and well-worn trainers. 'I wanted to come,' he said earnestly. 'I felt I ought to.' His shoulders slumped. 'Though what good it'll do now.' He left the sentence hanging before bursting out, 'Oh, what's the point?'

'Callum deserves representation,' Martha said quietly. 'And I think his mother would appreciate it.'

Adam Farthing managed a smile. 'Ah yes,' he said. 'The lovely Shelley.' He looked down at his shoes.

Martha waited. Adam Farthing had come here of his own volition. Probably Shelley Hughes had persuaded him. No mother could bear to see her son go to his grave without some sort of tribute being made.

Shall Life renew these bodies? Of a truth all death shall he annul?

Adam Farthing peered up at her. His head was habitually bowed so the movement seemed set at an uncomfortable angle, a swivelling, sideways turn. 'No one seems to want me to speak up for the lad,' he said hoarsely. 'My colleagues at the school have more or less warned me off.'

'Really?' Friends of Martha would have been alerted by the treacly tone in her voice. But Adam Farthing was a stranger. He continued – unaware.

'But he was good. He was a decent boy. If he hadn't been picked on.' His face screwed up. 'I can't help feeling responsible.'

'Responsible?'

She felt a quick, hot anger towards this weak, apologetic man. Had he never heard the rhyme 'For want of a nail'? Did he not see how these tragic events should have been nipped in the bud. And then there would have been no death.

'I suppose your colleagues are anxious to have no slur on the school,' she probed quietly.

'That plus a feeling of guilt that we stood by and did nothing.' For the first time she met Farthing's eyes and her dislike of him began to melt. He couldn't help being the sort of person he was. Like Callum Hughes he too was inherently decent.

'When did it start?'

'A year. No. Two years ago. I get the feeling Roger Gough… DreadNought…' A whisper of a smile broadened his mouth. 'Callum and I thought up the name between us. He was very 'in' to the First World War. Loved reading about the battles – the Somme, Ypres, Passchendaele, Ploegsteert, Loos, Serre.'

Martha felt a jolt. She had seen Callum Hughes mentally as an unfortunate and a criminal, *physically* as a frightened youth being marched down a corridor by two prison officers. She had seen him too as a corpse, a suicide victim. But this was the first time she had pictured him as someone real, someone with intelligence and identity, sympathy and interest in past events. She eyed the teacher.

He was still smiling at the memory. 'We thought the name, DreadNought, fitted him rather well. Huge great warship, you know. And Gough's a very overweight young man.' He gave a wry chuckle. 'Although I suspect the dread nought bit is a compliment. Like lots of bullies Gough is actually a bit of a coward. Take his cheerleaders away from him and he would soon have crumpled. But Gough was smart. He was careful he never was alone.' The brown eyes, tired with guilt, met hers and she knew that Callum's teacher would never quite forget his pupil. 'Gough was a thoroughly nasty piece of work, Mrs Gunn, a pull-the-legs-off-flies sort of boy. You know what I mean?'

'I do.'

'On the other hand young Callum – well – with his asthma and everything he was skinny. Bound to be the butt of jokes. They called him a Mother's Boy, teased him relentlessly. And Callum was a sensitive lad. He took it badly. And yet he was far from being the only one in the class to come from a single-parent home. Practically *de rigueur* in our school. But even the fact that his mum was alone seemed to mark him.' He broke off. 'You've met Shelley Hughes I suppose?'

'Yes.'

'Well – she's not the ordinary—' She caught a flash of the shy smile again. 'She's not your average single mum. There's a bit of something about her.'

Privately Martha agreed. But they were getting nowhere. It was time to rein him in. 'Why was nothing done to stop the bullying?'

'We tried. We did try but Shelley wouldn't make a formal complaint and Callum would just shrug and mutter. For him he became quite uncommunicative. He retreated. He wouldn't even confide in me. It was as though his fear of what was happening paralysed him. He couldn't seem to do anything about it – even enlist my help. It was impossible for us to take any action without evidence. The Goughs would have made mincemeat out of us. Taken us to court and accused us of defaming their son's character. Mr and Mrs Gough were convinced that their son was blameless and that if he attacked Callum then Callum must have provoked him. And, of course, subsequent events only reinforced their stance. No, Mrs Gunn. You might think right triumphs but in my experience it is the strongest and the one who shouts the loudest who wins, particularly when they have nothing to lose.'

'So you mentioned the bullying to Mr and Mrs Gough?'

Farthing looked almost embarrassed. 'In a very roundabout way. At a parents' evening I simply said that there was some bullying in the school, did they know anything about it?'

'Their response?'

'They just looked blank, said their son had nothing to do with any bullying, neither did he know anything about it, that just because he was big didn't make him a bully and why weren't his history marks higher, what did I have against him, why did I always mark him down? You get the picture?'

She nodded. 'And you never spoke to Gough yourself?'

'I didn't dare. Not without proper evidence. I let him know that I knew what was going on. I made hints and allusions, said things like I kept an eye on the playground during lunchtime. It was all I could do to protect young Callum. Anything more would have made him more of a teacher's pet.'

'You let him know that you were aware what he was doing but would do nothing about it?'

No answer.

'In my book that's a sort of tacit acquiescence, isn't it?'

Adam Farthing dropped his head again to stare at his trainers. They were old, worn and grubby.

'Don't make me feel worse,' he said. 'I didn't come here for criticism.'

'I come to bury Caesar, not to praise him,' she muttered, 'except you're doing the opposite.'

He smiled at her and for that brief second they shared something which seemed to give the teacher the confidence to say what had been on his mind.

'I need you to tell me what's appropriate to say at the inquest.'

Martha drew in a deep sigh and threw back her shoulders. She wanted to inspire him. 'Paint a picture of him, Mr Farthing. Speak up and say what his interests were, what his hobbies were, his sense of humour, what he did with his leisure time. Think of nice things, good things that his class mates have said about him.'

She knew instantly she'd said the wrong thing when Farthing's face changed and she filled in…

Psycho. Madman. Mad-Axe-Hughes. Killer. Murderer. Blood-letter.

How cruel it all was.

'We should have done something to stop it,' he said. 'We knew Roger Gough was a thug. I watched him through the windows. Taunting youngsters. Smacking them. Pushing them. One day I saw him shove Callum right into the road. A bus was coming. Gough's friends were all cheering. I thought then a tragedy would come from it. I rapped the window.' He paused as though he knew how inadequate this seemed. 'But even then I didn't foresee this.'

'What would you have done if you had?'

'Risked it,' Farthing said quietly. 'Got Gough suspended. I saw the incident. I knew it was dangerous. I knew the violence was escalating but I didn't do anything. I'll have to live with that for the rest of my life, Mrs Gunn.'

There is nothing I can do, Martha thought. You're right. You should have spoken out. You should have defended him. He was weak. Gough was strong. And now Callum is dead and Gough injured.

Farthing recovered and continued.

'Callum was an unusual boy – from the first. He absolutely loved history. In fact he had an insight into past events that was quite mature. He might have been a historian. His particular interest was the First World War. He read every book on the subject he could get his hands on. He even studied the poets, seemed to know how the soldiers had felt – all the futility, all the pointlessness. Everything.'

How ironic then that he should share an equally premature, untimely and violent death but how much more ignominious.

'He would have been a great person.'

'Perhaps.'

'Look,' she said. 'I'm glad that you've come. Make a brief speech, by all means, but no benefit can come now from talking about the bullying. You could perhaps say that Callum's life was not easy – or that many young people of today have a difficult time with friends and school. Talk about his interest in the First World War. You might even find a quotation from one of the poets which seems fitting.' She stood up.

'I'll see you next Tuesday then.'

She shook his hand.

Agnetha left for London on the Saturday morning, looking very attractive in a long white gypsy skirt, slung low over her narrow hips, a huge leather buckled belt emphasising her slimness. 'I'll be back Sunday night, Mrs Gunn,' she said gaily and accelerated the small Peugeot down the drive, her long arm jingling with huge bracelets waving out of the window until she was out of sight.

Martha enjoyed the Saturday night, for once alone with her daughter, poring over a Jamie Oliver recipe book for their teatime treat before settling down to a DVD of *Notting Hill* – Sukey's choice.

On Sunday she and Sukey were in the car by eleven, ready for their trip to see Sam. Martha had the mother's compulsion to take a tuck box full of goodies but she was unsure of what to put in it. Like many youngsters obsessed with sport, Sam was very fussy about what calories he ate. In the end she took a home-made parkin out of the freezer and trusted he would find it acceptable.

Liverpool colours were everywhere, she thought, as she drove into the academy. Lads carrying footballs were scurrying here and there, all with some purpose. She found Sam sitting in the reception and was glad when he couldn't hide his pleasure at seeing her. He was wearing Bermuda shorts, socks slipping down. Bruises on his right shin. He stood up and hugged her tightly. 'Hi Mum.'

She held him at arm's length and studied him. He was – reassuringly – the same Sam. Spiky hair, crooked teeth, tentative grin.

'Good gracious,' she said, maternal instinct to the fore. 'Don't you wear shin pads?'

'Mine slipped,' he said quickly.

She dropped the subject.

'So how's it going?'

'OK,' he said cautiously. 'Shall we go for a walk around?'

She nodded and again felt pleasure at the sight of the twins' heads together, Sukey's blonde hair looking even paler beside Sam's darker head with its suspicious tinge of red. 'I've told my roommates about my sister, the Abba fan,' she heard him say.

'Oh, I'm getting more sophisticated these days,' she replied, tossing her hair. 'I think my Abba phase is coming to an end.'

'I wouldn't have left home if I'd have known,' Sam said gruffly. 'I might have stuck it, Dancing Queen.'

Sukey pushed him sideways. 'Don't be such a freak,' she said kindly.

Martha let them wander ahead while she took in their surroundings. The pitches were immaculately kept, the grass looking like an advert for Green Things or something that sorted your lawns, killed the weeds, fed the grass. Everywhere she could hear encouragement from the Coaches, the odd scolding, a few shouts from the boys. 'Donnelly. Pass. Here. Over here, Bugall.' And on all the youngsters' faces was the same gritty determination she'd so often seen in Sam.

She caught up with them. 'So what was with the mistletoe code?'

Sam flushed. 'Nothing really, Mum. A bit of ragging from the others. And I suppose I was, well – it's a big thing moving out when you're just a teenager.'

'And?' she coaxed gently.

'I made a bit of an idiot of myself in the game,' he said dejectedly. 'And then I thought that's all I'm here for – the game. It's all any one cares about here. All they talk about. It seems strange. That's all. And if I don't play well no one forgets.' He was frowning. 'By coming here I've shut some pretty big doors, haven't I? Career-wise.'

She smiled. 'Not at thirteen, Sam.'

'I keep thinking if I don't perform well I'll be dropped. And then what?'

'Then you'll just have to get on with your life.'

Her son gave her a withering look.

So already he was in the frame. Something in Martha exulted while at the same time another part of her died.

It was a happy day, in general. She watched her son pick his food, choosing carefully, munching on pasta and salad. They left at eight and Martha felt reassured.

CHAPTER NINE

The inquest on Callum Hughes was held on the following Tuesday and as Martha had anticipated there was a large crowd outside an hour before it was due to begin. She pulled her Audi into the parking space and cast her eye around.

Reflecting her mood accurately it was pouring with rain, a dull day smothered in thick grey cloud. She fished her umbrella out from under the back seat and threw the door open. Immediately a microphone was pushed towards her. She appealed to the blonde, female reporter. 'Come on. Be reasonable. You know full well that anything I have to say I'll say inside. Let me get on with the inquest and you'll have your story.'

She was always ambivalent about the Press. It was a great servant but a terrible master. Anything you said on record could be twisted and cut so it sounded as though you'd said something completely different.

And yet coroners could serve a useful purpose, drawing attention to potentially lethal situations to bring about social change. Childproof tops on toxic substances had resulted from a toddler who had died as a result of ingesting bleach. They had argued for the wearing of compulsory seatbelts after hearing terrible details of wrecked faces and bodies which had been propelled through windscreens. It had been a coroner who had suggested the removal of toxic wadding in sofas after a series of children dying of smoke inhalation in tragic house fires. Because of its awful finality sometimes death can achieve something that life never could. Coroners are the mouthpieces of the dead.

As she mounted the steps to the court she was reflecting how she could add to the list of changes wrought by untimely death. Her own dilemma was that although Callum's death was certainly suicide there had been a chain of events which had led up to it. So should she now draw attention to that lethal sequence of circumstances and even perhaps hope that something would be done about it? Perhaps.

Jericho was waiting for her in the hallway wearing his one and only court suit with an appropriately grave expression on his face. 'Mrs Hughes is in the ante-room.' His voice too was in a hushed tone.

Had Jericho Palfreyman not been a coroner's assistant, she mused, he would have made a very good undertaker. Perhaps the jobs were not so far apart. She pushed the door open.

Shelley Hughes was standing up when Martha entered, and as soon she turned around Martha knew she had been crying. Her eyes were swollen and her mouth limp and quivering. She waited. Shelley sniffed and blew her nose on a well-used tissue. She managed the tiniest of smiles and crumpled the tissue in her hand as though she was trying to hide it. She was wearing no make-up. It made her look very pale and very young.

'How are you?'

Shelley snorted out an answer. 'How do you think?'

Then she seemed to remember that Martha was on her side.

'Lonely,' she said. 'I miss him. Every day just after four-fifteen, the time when he used to get home I think I hear him.' She squeezed her eyes tight shut to stop the tears. It didn't work. They rolled down her cheeks, dripped off her chin. 'I never thought I could feel so awful,' she said. 'I never thought my mind could go round and round the same events. I keep going over and over every single thing he said, wondering over and over again what I could have done.' Her fists were tightly clenched. She beat them against her sides. 'What could I have done? I don't know.'

Her hands had shredded the tissue and small flakes were falling to the ground. 'I have no future, Mrs Gunn. It's destroyed. Toxic waste.'

There are all sorts of platitudes for this sort of situation and in her time Martha had probably trotted them all out – sermons about time being a great healer, about something coming along in the future, that good could come out of bad, that grievers should move on. But to have said any one of those useful phrases would have been an insult to the raw grief Shelley Hughes was experiencing so Martha said nothing, merely watching her until the worst flood of grief had passed.

'Remember, Mrs Hughes, this inquest is about your son's suicide not about the assault. We're not concerned with the circumstances which led up to your son's being at Stoke Heath only what led up to his death.' Martha touched her arm. 'It's better that way,' she said. 'If we focus on the tragedy of your son's death it will be kinder than if you speak about the part others played in his incarceration.' She needed to know. 'Do you understand?'

Shelley Hughes nodded and they walked into the courtroom together.

Martha opened the inquest in the accepted formal fashion.

They began with the two police officers who had accompanied Callum to the magistrates' court. Martha had already read their separate statements and thought it best if PC Gethin Roberts spoke for both of them. He was smartly turned out in full and polished uniform, his helmet tucked under his arm as he approached the witness box. But even the uniform couldn't hide his nervousness.

He read from a statement beginning with the Tuesday afternoon and his arrival at the school. Martha imagined, just for a moment, the mayhem which must have followed Callum's assault on his schoolmate. The screaming ambulance, the hysterical children, the agony of the boy and in the middle, thin, pale and almost certainly shocked, Callum himself, hardly knowing what he had done.

'He did not resist arrest,' Roberts said. 'We took him to Monkmoor police station where he was put into the care of the custody sergeant.'

Sergeant Paul Talith was next to take the oath. He too looked uncomfortable. Martha watched him carefully. The coroner's court frequently did this to people, particularly in such a case, made them feel guilty – responsible.

She settled back in her seat.

'They handed Callum Hughes over to the custody officer at five-thirty,' he said solidly, 'while we called to collect his mother, him being a minor.'

'How did he seem,' Martha asked.

'He was in a state of shock. He seemed to be dazed, as

though he hardly knew what he'd done. We charged him with malicious wounding. We contacted the duty solicitor and collected his mother. The police surgeon pronounced him fit to detain.'

Shelley Hughes's shoulders twitched.

'He was very quiet during the questioning and we told him he'd be up in front of the magistrates in the morning. His mother left, as did the solicitor.'

'How did he seem,' Martha asked again.

'Still very quiet. As you'd expect. We gave him something to eat.'

Talith's eyes flicked around the court and Martha wondered whether he had felt any pity for the boy.

'How did Callum seem overnight in Shrewsbury police station?'

'He slept all right.'

There was a gasp from the back of the court. Martha looked up warily. She had expected scenes.

'Sergeant Talith,' she said, 'did he say anything that would have led you to believe he might be a suicide risk?'

Talith scratched the back of his neck. 'He didn't say anything, your honour, but we keep a close eye on all our detainees. Callum had had a shocking day. That was enough.'

There was another gasp from the gallery. A woman had shot to her feet.

'A shocking day,' she screamed, 'what about my lad? I call that shocking.'

She was appealing to the entire gallery. 'What he did to my boy. He doesn't deserve your sympathy.'

Martha banged her gavel once. 'Silence please. Sit down.

This is the inquest for the tragic death of a young teenager.'

'Tragic?' Another voice from the back of the gallery. Male this time. 'God rot his soul.'

'If you can't be silent,' Martha said, 'I shall have to order the police to clear the court.'

It worked – for now.

Talith continued. 'In the morning he showered and put on some clean clothes. He had his breakfast and we drove him to the magistrates' court.'

There was another angry gasp and Martha shot a warning glance towards the back row of the gallery. This time it was enough.

All this time she had avoided looking directly at Shelley Hughes but now she looked down at the front row. Shelley was wearing a black suit. And even her neat figure and pretty face couldn't disguise the fact that it was a cheap black suit, the skirt very slightly too short with a puckered hem. She was sitting very still, looking very alone, on an empty row.

She looked small and hunched and vulnerable which made Martha reflect that perhaps Callum's vulnerability had come from his mother.

Behind Shelley, also alone, sat Adam Farthing – almost unrecognisable in a neat, charcoal suit. His hair had been combed and trimmed. He wore what was surely a university tie – blue with a narrow yellow stripe and a badge in the middle. Martha couldn't see his feet but at a guess his footwear today wasn't the scruffy trainers. There was something very different in his manner. He sat, composed, staring straight ahead. Looking so different Martha almost wondered whether it was the same person. He looked an academic.

Deaths have a ripple effect and sometimes the waves lap into far and unexpected corners.

Martha resumed the inquest. 'Can you complete your statement please, Sergeant Talith?'

Talith looked out into the courtroom. 'He was perfectly polite. Very quiet and he said nothing about wanting to kill himself.'

'Did Callum injure himself at any time?'

'No, Ma'am.'

'And did you need to apply restraint?'

The answer was the same. 'No, Ma'am.'

'Thank you, Sergeant.'

The policeman stepped down from the witness box, his shoes squeaking as he walked. In another place it could have been funny but here no one was laughing – or even smiling.

Talith sat down again, his heavy form causing the chair to creak as he lowered into it.

It too sounded terribly loud in the silence of the court.

'This is a load of nonsense.'

An obese man wearing a Black Sabbath T-shirt had jumped to his feet. 'The guy was a psycho. He killed himself because he was a psycho.'

Shelley Hughes had frozen on the bench as the man appealed to everyone in the court.

Martha banged the gavel again and ordered the police to clear the public gallery.

Minutes later the gallery had been cleared and Martha heaved a sigh of relief. But this in itself was a mixed blessing.

It meant that the papers could string out different headlines. 'Protests at Coroner's Court. Angry scenes' and so on. And if she knew the Press they'd be busily taking comments from the mob outside.

But it also had a downside. It robbed the papers of their chance to portray Callum Hughes not as a knife-wielding psychopath but as a flesh and blood person, someone who had a life other than when he stuck a knife into a school fellow. Martha had followed the story in both the national and the local papers and the angle they had unanimously taken had been that this had been an 'unprovoked attack' by a quiet and strange boy. Without actually saying the words they had already sown the seeds that Callum Hughes had had some mental disorder – psychopathy, schizophrenia. It didn't really matter which. In the media all mental illness is lumped together. They are all weirdos.

The police surgeon was next to be called. Delyth Fontaine. Unruffible, professional. She lumbered up to the witness stand, her hair grey and dry, wearing a huge peasant skirt of muted browns and creams. Delyth had a presence. No one could be indifferent to her. She was invariably noticed. She gave her evidence concisely, anticipating exactly what Martha would need to know.

'I saw Callum Hughes on the Tuesday evening,' she said, 'at about eight o'clock. I pronounced him fit for detainment.'

Martha interrupted. 'When you pronounced him fit for detainment did you examine him physically?'

'No. Callum had no complaints. He appeared well. There was no reason for me to examine him.'

'So you are unable to tell me whether he had any injuries?'

'None that he complained of.'

A more junior police surgeon might have baulked under the omission but Delyth Fontaine was sure of her ground.

'Did you form any opinion about the boy's mental state?'

The police surgeon hesitated for a split second and could not prevent her eyes from sliding towards the boy's mother.

'He was calm,' she said. 'Frightened but calm.'

'Did you deem him a suicide risk?'

Again the police surgeon seemed to take the time to consider the question afresh. 'No,' she said, 'at least not particularly. As with all young offenders, particularly first time young offenders who have committed a violent crime, I would warn the custody officers to take careful watch.'

'Did you in this case?'

Again the split-second hesitation. 'Truthfully,' she said, 'I cannot remember in this specific case. All I can say is that in these circumstances it is my usual practice.'

In the front row Shelley Hughes's shoulders drooped a bit lower.

The police surgeon had probably picked up on the movement. She addressed her next sentence to Shelley Hughes. 'I think I would have done,' she said firmly.

She continued. 'I did not see him again until the Thursday morning, at seven-thirty, when I pronounced him dead. A computer cable had been looped around his neck in a slip-knot. When I saw him he was lying on the floor. I understood the prison officers had found him in a hanging position and had cut him down.' She spoke coldly and with a professional detachment but something crossed her face – some hesitation, some brief moment to think. Martha had known Doctor

Fontaine ever since she had first come to Shrewsbury, more than ten years ago, and this was one of the times when she had read some sympathy for a victim. Delyth glanced across at her. She was frowning.

Martha could have pressed her as to the cause of death but Mark Sullivan was sitting on the second row, yards away from Adam Farthing. He had slipped in about half an hour ago.

Don't mess this up, Martha thought. At least do the boy the courtesy of representing him sober.

What would young Callum have made of all this, Martha wondered? All these people from diverse occupations, some of whom he had never met, others with whom he had had the briefest of glancing encounters and yet others part of his everyday existence, like the Gough family who ranted outside and his mother and teacher who sat inside, openly grieving for him.

What would the boy who had loved early twentieth-century history, who had been let down by the people who should have protected him, cowed by the criminal justice system, bullied to the point where he had snapped, sharpened a knife with one intent, studied the terrible slaughter of the First World War while marvelling at the talent it had both unearthed and destroyed, what would he have made of today's proceedings?

Martha dismissed Delyth Fontaine and called on the senior of the two Reliant van drivers who worked for the prison transport system and had taken Callum from the magistrates' court in Shrewsbury to his final destination, the Young Offenders' Institute at Stoke Heath. There was no point in calling both of them. She had read their statements.

Andrew Witherspoon was one of the Group 4 Security officers. He was a stolid, Shropshire potato of a man, about thirty years old, with shrewd blue eyes. The first part of his statement was concerned with dry details and he read it through quickly.

'We picked Callum Hughes up just before nine o'clock in the evening. We'd had a busy day bringing some inmates down from Walton prison so were a bit later than we'd like to have been. He was handed over by PC Roberts. Callum was very quiet and raised no objection to our transporting him. We asked him if he was OK to come and he acquiesced.' The Reliant officer flushed self-consciously at his use of the unfamiliar word and his quick blue eyes scanned the court to check that everyone had heard it before continuing.

'We did not need to restrain him. The road was quiet. He was a bit travel sick. The journey took thirty-five minutes. My colleague sat in the back with him. Callum stayed quiet and seemed to accept where he was going and what would happen to him. He did not seem distressed. On arrival at Stoke Heath we handed him over to Prison Officer Walton Pembroke and then we left. We did not see Callum again and he did not, at any time, express an intention to take his own life. He seemed,' his eyes drifted across the front seats – empty except for the one, lonely woman. His eyes focused directly on her. 'He seemed a nice lad.'

Shelley Hughes lifted her eyes. They were brimming with tears. She gave a confused nod in the general direction of Andrew Witherspoon. Martha knew she was savouring these sweet words about her boy.

Witherspoon's eyes met Martha's. 'Did Callum suffer any

injuries while he was with you – perhaps a jolt in the van?'

Witherspoon knew exactly what he was being asked. 'No, Ma'am.'

'Thank you.'

Maybe now was a good time for a break.

It was also a good opportunity to have a private word with Shelley Hughes.

The gap between her teeth seemed more pronounced – or perhaps it was that her face had lost weight. Her complexion looked grey.

'I call the prison officers next and then the pathologist, Shelley.'

Shelley Hughes nodded and Martha wished she had someone with her. Anyone – husband, brother, sister, mother. Did she have any idea of the type of evidence Mark Sullivan would give?

'It can be quite hard, Mrs Hughes.'

Shelley opened her lips. They moved but she said nothing.

'I'll keep his evidence to a minimum.'

This time Shelley Hughes managed a mumbled 'yes.'

Jericho bustled in with two cups of tea and handed them out.

Shelley drank hers quickly.

'Did Callum have any special friends?'

'Uum.'

'Did friends never call round for him, ring him up? Did he have a mobile phone?'

'Yes. Pay as you go. He used it for games most of the time.'

'It might be an idea if you checked it, Shelley. There must

have been a few friends somewhere.'

Shelley's face twisted. 'Maybe there were but it was like leprosy having DreadNought against you. You caught it. And then you were part of it. Anyone who befriended Callum was running the risk of being in the same boat as him. Understand?'

Martha nodded.

Shelley put her mug down. 'Shall we get on?' She managed a smile. 'It's not going to get any easier, is it?'

Martha watched the prison officer give evidence and thought what a tough man he was. Sure of himself, confident in his job. There was nothing new in his statement and he too denied having to use any restraint on Callum – apart from having to manhandle him back into his cell.

And that, Martha decided, would not account for the boy's injuries.

'Did you keep a suicide watch on him?'

The prison officer shrugged. 'We looked through the spyhole a couple of times. Then he seemed asleep. We decided a close, suicide watch was unnecessary.'

'Is there a possibility that he could have been feigning sleep?'

Pembroke shrugged again. 'It's possible,' he admitted. 'But how would we know unless we actually entered the cell, which would disturb him?'

Martha nodded and Pembroke sat down, next to Stevie Matthews who was patently finding her first inquest daunting. She looked terrified.

Mark Sullivan looked smaller than when she had last seen him. But surely it is not possible for a man to shrink in less than a week? He looked dehydrated, wrinkled.

He took the stand with an odd reluctance, swearing the oath with the same unwillingness. She watched him curiously. Something was troubling him.

As usual he began with the dry facts, time and place of post-mortem, formal identification by the boy's mother. Place of death. Then he listed the boy's injuries. 'I noted the mark of a ligament around the boy's neck, some petechial haemorrhaging on the eyelids. I also noted bruising around the right orbit and cheek, blood in the left nostril – possibly sustained at around the time of death. A large bruise on the shin – almost certainly sustained a few hours before death.' Martha encouraged Sullivan to enlarge with a nod. At the same time she saw Shelley Hughes lean forward, take a pad from her handbag and start writing. She was taking notes.

'I was of the opinion that the bruising on the shin was sustained a few hours before death because there was extensive bruising and tissue leakage around the area. I deduced that if time of death had been some time between twelve midnight when the prison officers saw him alive and six-thirty when he was discovered by his cell mate that the shin injury had probably been sustained shortly after he was confined to his cell.'

Shelley Hughes was scribbling rapidly.

'When my colleague, Doctor Fontaine, examined Callum's body his core temperature was 31 degrees with an ambient temperature of 22. I would therefore put his time of death as being very shortly after midnight. Callum was a very slim young man and cooling is accelerated in the thin. However I would stress that this is a rough guide only.'

Martha nodded her approval.

'In addition to the above injuries I noted some bruising on the front and side aspect of the chest which had probably been sustained an hour or two before he died.'

So this was the reason for Mark Sullivan's reluctance to testify, Martha thought. Two injuries severe enough to have marked the boy's body which happened at some time between him arriving at Stoke Heath and hanging himself.

She took a swift glance at Shelley Hughes and knew that the boy's mother realised fully the significance of what she was hearing.

Sullivan's evidence posed two questions for her. What relevance did these other injuries have to the boy's cause of death and so her verdict and two, should she adjourn the inquest pending police enquiry into the two separate injuries? She took a swift glance at Callum's mother and knew she would fight every inch of the way. She was a fighting tigress for her young. Not his life now but simply justice.

She tried to pre-empt Shelley's response.

'Doctor Sullivan, do you believe these injuries had any bearing on the boy's final cause of death?'

'No.'

But another swift glance at Callum's mother confirmed what she had already thought.

Mark Sullivan went on to give the findings of the post-mortem. 'My findings during post-mortem were consistent with hanging from a low point of suspension,' he said, 'such as the side rail of the upper bunk as shown to me by the prison officers at Stoke Heath. In my experience death is almost instantaneous. There was nothing to suggest a felony had

taken place. Neither was there any suggestion that Callum
Hughes had been coerced into taking his own life. It appeared
that shortly after the prison officers had checked him he had
been overcome with emotion and decided to take his own
life.'

Shelley Hughes was wearing a stubborn look. The grief and
numbness were wearing off to be replaced by a slow and
vengeful anger which Martha sensed.

'We'll take a break now,' she said.

With his usual skill Jericho had organised coffee and
sandwiches for her. Martha handed the plate to Shelley who
took one and started eating.

'In my opinion,' Martha said cautiously, 'there isn't any
doubt that Callum killed himself,' she said

'But why,' Shelley demanded. 'Everyone says that Callum
didn't say anything about killing himself.'

'Come on,' Martha said gently. 'You know he said he might
as well be dead.'

Shelley touched her arm. 'But he didn't say he would, did
he? Why? That's the question. And how did he get those
bruises on his leg and the rest of him? That hasn't been
explained, has it? Maybe that's why he killed himself, because
the psycho they put him in with duffed him over, didn't he?
He went for him. And my Call thought he couldn't go along
with that for a couple of years. Maybe he spoke to the prison
officers, asked them if he could be moved or something. Ask
them if he did. And then even if he'd have survived the years
in prison what future would he have had? People would have
ganged up against him, wouldn't they? He'd have been

infamous. Everyone would have known him as the psycho what knifed a school friend.'

It was undeniable.

'That's why he did it and I want you to ask the right people the right questions.'

'Shelley,' Martha said softly. 'I can close the inquest now if you like. Death by suicide. We can say there were extenuating factors if you like. Then you can go ahead and have the funeral.'

'No. It's my last chance to do right by my boy. I'm not taking the easy way out. When he went to school that morning he didn't have any bruises on him. Now then – if DreadNought had gone for him that day Call would have been up in front of the courts on a charge of self defence.'

Martha frowned. 'The bruises happened after he was taken into custody.'

'And how exact a science is it?'

Martha knew the answer. Forensics is rarely an exact science at all.

She eyed Shelley. *I see, she thought. A woman on a mission.*

'I want to do what's best for you – and Callum,' she said calmly. 'If you want we can adjourn the inquest pending police enquiry.'

Slowly Shelley nodded. 'That's what I want,' she said, 'after we've heard Mr Farthing speak.'

Martha nodded.

'I want those injuries explained satisfactorily.'

Martha couldn't argue. Faced with Shelley Hughes's determined fury she felt powerless.

'I want everything to come out. Every little stone picked up and turned over. If he asked the prison officers to move him and they didn't so he hanged himself I want them implicated. And if my boy was assaulted by his cell mate I want charges to be pressed.' Shelley gave a smile. 'I want justice for my son.'

Martha caught up with Alex Randall as he was re-entering the court. 'You're going to have to question Tyrone Smith again, Alex. Mrs Hughes wants a full enquiry into how Callum got those bruises.'

He nodded.

'She won't let things settle. I'm going to have to adjourn the inquest after his teacher's given his speech. She's also got it into her head that Callum asked the prison officers to move him from cell 101, away from Tyrone Smith.'

Again he nodded.

'And I suppose the Gough family are outside, waiting to hiss and boo her?'

'We can take her out of the back door if you like.'

'I think that would be a good idea.'

They smiled at each other.

Adam Farthing made a good impression on the court. His voice was soft and well toned. He had a command he had lacked when he had spoken to Martha and she caught a glimpse of an inspired and competent teacher.

'I'm here today,' he started diffidently, 'because I knew Callum Hughes very well. He was a pupil of mine for a number of years, since he was eight years old, in fact. I taught him history which was his favourite subject. Like most historians he had a favourite period, the First World War.' He shot a glance at Martha. 'Callum was not religious, as far as I know, but I would like to read out a tiny piece from a poem by his favourite war poet – Wilfred Owen – himself a Shropshire lad, who also died terribly, tragically young.

Move him into the sun –

> Gently its touch awoke him once,
> At home, whispering of fields half sown.
> Always it woke him, even in France,
> Until this morning and this snow.
> If anything will wake him now
> The kind old sun will know.

He closed his book.

'Callum would have liked it,' he said, 'and I can't think Wilfred Owen would have minded my borrowing his words.'

With that he left the stand with dignity and walked back to his seat while Shelley Hughes watched with rapt attention, as though the history teacher was delivering a divine sermon.

Martha too felt the strange, peaceful reluctance to move which had always washed over her when her father had taken her on a Sunday evening to listen to the sermon at the Methodist church.

CHAPTER TEN

On the Friday Roger Gough died.

Martha got the call late in the evening from a hesitant doctor at the hospital and listened, stunned.

The doctor was defensive. 'It was always a serious injury,' he started. 'When he was admitted we realised it would be touch and go.'

'What did he actually die of?'

'Complications. Infection. He had a pneumothorax then finally a pulmonary embolus. We anticoagulated but it was no good.'

She let the doctor continue. 'He got a massive infection,' he said, 'which caused major organ failure. We used every known antibiotic but pneumonia set in. The wound had punctured his lung and we had real trouble drawing the pneumothorax and his condition deteriorated. He didn't have a chance. He wasn't fit for surgery. We did all we could but in the end we lost him.'

She thanked him for the information and replaced the receiver.

So now she had another set of grieving relatives to deal with. But the Goughs were not like Shelley Hughes. They were angry and aggressive.

And she could well understand their fury. They had watched their son die gradually, in front of their eyes – watched the doctors struggle to save his life and witnessed the defeat.

The post-mortem on Roger Gough was held early on the Saturday morning and she'd asked Mark Sullivan to ring her with his findings. She'd decided not to attend. She simply couldn't face watching another thirteen-year-old be subjected to a pathologist's knife.

The findings were as expected.

'The chest wound was deep,' he said. 'Very close to the heart. It had touched the inferior vena cava but not punctured it. They'd have made much of this had the other lad lived. Incidentally Roger Gough had a degree of cardiomegaly. I suspect his heart was enlarged due to obesity. He certainly wasn't a sporty boy. The cause of death was major organ failure due to a pulmonary embolus due to stasis due to the original chest wound. There was one other surprising finding,' he said. 'Gough was what – thirteen years old? He had atherosclerosis. He was a porky fellow with quite a deposit of fat around his heart. He was in really poor physical condition. Worrying in such a young lad.'

'But there's no doubt about it, Mark? He died as a direct result of the assault.'

"Fraid so,' he said. 'No doubt about it. As I said, if the other boy had lived no clever lawyer could have got him off.'

So she would have no option but to return a verdict of homicide.

The weekend papers led with the story of the second boy's

death, the front pages holding school pictures of both of them: Roger Gough smiling confidently into the camera, Callum looking nervous, his mouth twisted and his eyes fearful as though someone stood behind the photographer. Had the captions not labelled them, *Killer* and *Victim,* you would have sworn the story would have unfolded the other way round. Callum *looked* a victim. Both must have done their mothers proud in their school blazers and ties and crisp white shirts.

Nowhere was Gough referred to as a bully or Callum as a victim. It was all the other way round with the newspapers directing their readers' sympathy. Callum was portrayed as a cold-blooded killer and Gough as a popular member of the form. So Callum Hughes's name was further vilified. But what drew Martha's attention was the quote by Katie Ashbourne, described as Gough's girlfriend. 'Callum was sort of jealous of Roger. 'Cause Roger was good at sport and quite clever and that and had loads of mates but Call – well – he was sort of on his own. All the time on his own. He weren't a good mixer.' (This sparked off another flurry of headlines about Callum Hughes being a 'loner' with all that that implied.)

'I knew one day they'd have a big fall out but I never thought it would be like that. I never thought Call would knife him.'

(The girlfriend who never thought tragedy would happen).

'I saw what happened. Call had such a look on his face. Sort of mad-like. I've had to have counselling since 'cos I kept having nightmares about it.'

Another 'friend' was quoted as saying that Callum was a loner, a Chelsea Arnold, but, and this caused Martha to sit up, Ms Arnold was described as a friend to both boys.

Martha leaned back in her chair and put the paper back down on the table. What was the girl talking about? Good at sport when Mark Sullivan had found fatty deposits round the boy's heart. She picked up the paper again and peered at the school picture of Gough, studied his lardy face.

Was she the only one who could spot the flaw in the girl's story?

So young Katie Ashbourne, Gough's girlfriend, was a liar.

How sad when she had been Callum Hughes's secret fantasy.

Martha leaned back, thinking. Then she sat forward.

She was sitting in Martin's study. And not for the first time it hit her how dark and old-fashioned it was. It was a nice room, south facing with french windows which led out into the garden – onto a large patio with tubs of roses, old English pink, scarlet floribunda, patio roses and her pride and joy: a huge flowerpot containing the yellow tea rose, Peace. Beyond the patio the lawn was peppered with fruit trees: apple, cherry and a damson. From a girl she had always wanted an orchard. Martha turned away from the window and looked back into the room, at the marble fireplace, the heavy, dark wallpaper, the thick curtains. She picked up a photograph of Martin, laughing, holding the twins. While the rest of the house had been decorated at regular intervals she had not touched this room since Martin's death. She had planned to, with Evelyn, but when Evelyn had died, she had, once again, lost heart. And so it had remained, in a way, her husband's shrine. But now she felt an overwhelming need to move on, to redecorate the room and move her study back into it.

She stared hard into Martin's face, almost asking for his

understanding. But all she noticed was that even then he had been starting to look tired and worn out. The picture had been taken just after he had started his first course of chemotherapy and it had knocked the stuffing out of him. She had spent weeks watching him struggle to stay awake while he sat in the leather armchair. He'd liked this one best because it had a soft seat and as he had shed weight most chairs had seemed too hard.

They had done their best to remain optimistic that he would watch their two, beautiful children, grow up but it had been hard. They had each had their own brand of realism: he a lawyer, she a doctor.

But it had not been like that.

Instead she had watched the twins grow up alone and for a long time had thought that life had been too cruel. But now she knew it was time to move on. She did not need to preserve this shrine any more. Martin would live on through his children. And she would buy magazines and look for ideas how best to decorate the room. She would visit Simon Boyd's, the material shop near the Welsh Bridge, scan the Period House Shop for cornices and paints. She started to plan and hum. And the planning and the humming gave her vibrant energy. She would transform this room from being a shrine to a garden room, bright and clean, welcoming in each season, spring and summer, autumn and winter. She would buy garden furniture and solar lights and throw the french windows wide open. She and Sukey and Agnetha would spend the winter poring over books on interior design, wallpaper books, check fabric samples, look at a new sofa or two. She would buy a really good stereo system and indulge her love of music. From popular classics to Sixties oldies and yes – Abba too.

And then when it was all finally done she would have a party.

She bustled around happily in the kitchen for the next hour, preparing tea – Welsh lamb chops with fresh French beans and new potatoes, garnished with mint and salty Welsh butter. Sukey seemed excited by the project and not saddened at all by the fact that the only masculine room in the entire house – apart from Sam's which was a Liverpool shrine – was about to be changed. And she said nothing about it being 'her Dad's room' or anything similar. She even went up to her room and searched on the Internet for some design ideas.

Agnetha arrived home a little after nine, giggling and sporting an aquamarine ring on the third finger of her left hand. 'He says he is missing me, Mrs Gunn. He asked me to marry him.' She shrugged her thin shoulders. 'Why should I say no?'

Sukey stared at her long and hard, realising the implication of Agnetha's new found status. Then she jumped to her feet and hugged her.

'And the nice thing is now, Mummy, I don't need an au pair any more. I'm old enough to take care of myself.'

Her household was being slowly eroded, Martha thought. First Sam then Agnetha. And one day it would be Sukey, off to college.

She was reflective as she went to bed.

The Goughs arrived at her office late on the Monday morning, bursting in behind Jericho without allowing him to announce them.

Christina Gough was a large woman with hair striped, part white, part mousy, part chocolate brown. It looked an amateur

job with uneven chunks of colour. She was dressed in designer-
torn jeans and orange top and accompanied by a large man of
about forty who was panting with the effort. He too was
dressed in jeans and a black, sleeveless T-shirt showing meaty
biceps. His face was red and he was sweating. Martha
recognised them both as the troublemakers from the inquest.

They looked less grief-stricken than furiously angry.

She sat them both down, Jericho supplied them with coffee
and she explained her role.

'We're his parents.' The man, wagging his finger at her,
spoke for the woman. 'And we want justice.'

'As I understand it, Mr Gough, the boy who assaulted your
son committed suicide. Surely?'

She couldn't finish the sentence.

If she had hoped to meliorate their anger by reminding
them of the facts it failed miserably.

Gough continued wagging his finger at her. 'We want
justice,' he said again.

'In what way, Mr Gough?'

By bringing the dead back to life so you can put him down
again? Not possible.

She allowed them to speak on.

'My son was a decent lad,' Gough's father said. 'He was
struck down by a psychopath. It's a bloody good job that the
little bleeder topped his self else I'd have done it for him. His
life wouldn't have been worth a farthing if he'd have got out.
As they do.' He sounded as though he was accusing her. ' I
want you to say that at the inquest.'

She recalled the bus incident when Gough had almost
pushed young Callum under its wheels. It could so easily have

been the other way round, she reflected, and felt herself shaking her refusal. 'There is no evidence to point to Callum Hughes as being a psychopath,' she said. 'He had no history of previous attacks on people. Only your son.' She had hoped they would draw their own conclusions from so pointed a remark but they drew the wrong one.

'I bet if we ask around we'll find someone else he went for. Buggers like that make a habit of it.'

His wife touched his arm. 'What about Katie? You heard he flashed at her? He was a perv.' Her voice rose. 'It's obvious, isn't it?'

'Yeah. Besides if he weren't a psychopath,' Gough said, 'why did he take a knife to our lad? Eh?' He wagged the finger at her again. 'Answer me that.'

'There's been mention of bad blood between the two boys,' Martha said cautiously. Mrs Gough spoke again. 'If there were bad blood,' she said, 'it were because the Hughes boy were a psycho and my lad knew it.' She sat back in her chair, folded her fat arms and looked pleased with herself.

'Are you saying that your son was frightened of Callum Hughes?'

Gough stood up. 'My lad weren't frightened of nothing,' he said.

'So he never voiced any concerns about the boy?'

Both Goughs shook their heads.

'The function of an inquest is simply to ascertain who has died, how, when and where. I'm not prepared to cast aspersions on Callum Hughes at your son's inquest. His mother has suffered enough but I can tell you that your son's death will be classed as homicide.'

Oddly enough the words seemed to upset both parents. Gough put his arm round his wife's meaty shoulders.

'Your son will have the dignity of an inquest as did the Hughes boy. This is a tragic incident. I'm sorry for your loss.'

Gough tried another tack. 'The hospital was negligent,' he said. 'They should have been able to keep him alive.'

Blame is a common feature of grief. Relatives of people who have died in hospital frequently complain that *something* should have been done. That their wife/husband/mother/son should *not* have died. Therefore it must be the hospital's fault. Martha could not even allow the thought to creep in that sometimes it is financial benefit which is the moralist.

'I bet he got that MRSA.'

'No,' Martha said. 'At no point did he develop MRSA. He was simply too ill to fight off *any* infection.'

Gough snorted, stood up and spoke to his wife. 'It's a cover-up,' he said. 'A conspiracy. She's no bloody good at all.' He turned to Martha then. 'What good can you do?'

Very little, Martha thought. I am not the Resurrection woman but a mouthpiece of the law and the dead.

Gough turned back to Martha, his face red with fury and frustration. 'You're no fucking good at all,' he said. 'Thanks. Thanks for exactly nothing. Come on, Chrissie. Bloody typical.' He was still muttering as he let the door swing behind them.

Martha felt depressed when they'd left. She sat down at her desk, not even deriving her usual pleasure from the sight of the town, rising like a crown out of the river, the spire of St Chad's its topmost point. It was a bright, September day. The sky was blue with a few fleecy clouds. Outside it was just starting to get chilly and when the wind blew one or two leaves drifted down lazily from the trees hinting at impending autumn. Nothing too threatening yet. It was her favourite time of year.

She stood up and crossed to the window for a minute or two until she was disturbed by a soft knock on the door. She smiled. Jericho with his eternal cups of coffee.

But she was wrong. Alex Randall stuck his head in. 'Is this a bad time? I was just passing and thought I'd pop in and see what was going on.'

'I'm glad to see you,' she said. "I've just had an uncomfortable time with the Gough parents who are angry at everyone – the Health Service, Callum Hughes. They're spitting blood. And they wanted me to explain how it was that their nice, innocent boy was knifed by this psycho and why won't I say that at the inquest.'

'Oh dear.' Alex lowered his long frame into the armchair. 'Well – I've just come from speaking to Tyrone Smith.'

'Not sure who I'd prefer to deal with. Not much of a choice really, is it? The Gough family or Smith. What did *he* have to say?'

'He admits kicking Callum on the shin but,' He grinned, 'and I quote '*I never touched 'is bleedin' face.*' He couldn't say whether when Callum arrived he had or complained for any facial trauma.'

'I suppose we'd already guessed that.' She chewed on her lip. 'You know, Alex.'

They were interrupted. This time it really was Jericho with two cups of coffee. Martha waited until he had closed the door behind him before continuing.

'I can't believe that Smith slept through Callum hanging himself. I just can't.'

'We-ell' Randall put his mug down on the table. 'I think we may have a sort of explanation for that.'

'Yes?'

'Smith had been quite troublesome at night. He couldn't sleep, suffered from nightmares, would repeatedly bang on his door, keeping everyone else awake. He was given sleeping tablets.'

'You're joking.'

Alex shook his head. 'Unfortunately not. They'd been prescribed for him by the prison doctor – a short course.'

'Which he'd have had trouble stopping,' Martha said wearily. 'But you're right. It does explain something which was making no sense.'

'Yes. Well it explains Callum's shin injury but not the bruises on his face and chest. If he's telling the truth. We need to get this right, Martha, and we're not there yet.'

'So where do you go from here?'

'I suppose I should talk to the two prison officers again.'

'Good. Once we can explain the injuries to Shelley Hughes's satisfaction we can complete the inquest. Both inquests. It'll be better for everyone if Callum is buried soon. Roger Gough too. But I have the feeling that Gough's parents are going to be very belligerent. I think they'll keep hunting for someone or something to blame. Someone to sue. I think his inquest will be a long, drawn out affair which will, in turn, keep the story cooking in the Press.'

'When is Roger Gough's inquest?'

'Next week. I'll have to return a verdict of homicide.'

Martha was rubbing her forehead.

'You all right?'

'Yes. My au pair's got engaged. She'll be leaving soon, I expect. Which'll leave me alone with Sukey.'

'You're not thinking of having another au pair?'

'Sukey doesn't want it. She feels grown up. But this job doesn't always have regular hours and as you know our house is tucked away on its own. I mean she's a sensible girl but I would prefer it if someone was there with her.'

Alex nodded but made no comment. He didn't say that it was a shame about Martin and he didn't ask her about a relationship.

Instead he said, 'And how's Sam getting on?'

Again she felt her brow furrow. 'I'm not sure. I *think* he's OK but boys don't always say, do they? The old roast beef for tea. I'm hungry.'

'Sorry?'

'Wilfred Owen,' she said, 'writing from the trenches. Hiding his real situation from his mother. That's boys for you, Alex. Girls are different.' The statement jogged her memory. 'By the way, did you read the paper yesterday?'

'Bits.'

'Specifically Katie Ashbourne's statement.'

'No, what did she say?'

'More or less what a psycho Callum was and what a nice guy Roger Gough was. Toeing the usual line.'

'Well, well,' he said. 'Given the circumstances it's understandable. She was DreadNought's girlfriend.'

They chatted for a bit longer before Alex stretched his legs out as though the sitting still was giving him cramp. 'Well –

I'd better move on. I just thought you'd want to know how our enquiries were progressing.'

'Thanks. What's next?'

'Back to the prison officers. As you said, until we've got a satisfactory explanation for the other bruises Shelley Hughes is not going to rest. And that means you won't be able to close the inquest.'

He left.

But when he'd gone Martha started pondering.

She was aware that her sympathies had remained with Callum Hughes. And because of that she felt a compulsion to present him as a victim who had spilled over into violence rather than as the instigator of events.

As for Gough she saw him now as another victim – of his attitudes and prejudices.

Her mind flicked back to the CCTV footage of Callum's last encounter with the two prison warders and the terror she had sensed in the boy even through the poor quality, grainy images. Superimposed on that was the testimony of Adam Farthing who had known both boys. He had painted a graphic enough portrait of Callum, bookish and thoughtful, and Gough, lashing out with his fists while enjoying both fear and accolade from his schoolmates.

Even the nickname Callum had dreamed up for Gough, the fear of nothing, the *DreadNought* warship and the picture that the name had conjured up, all had added to the myth of Roger Gough and made him bigger, tougher, more invincible than he was.

Two teenage boys were dead and nothing would change. The school would continue teaching, boys and girls would still be bullied. There would still be weak and strong, the one taking cruel advantage of the other. There would always be stupid and intelligent. And so on.

It still happened at the school where murdered and victim had attended?

She sat back and struggled with her conscience. Sometimes her role as coroner was not quite enough. These were the times when she did a little probing for herself – as Martha *Rees*. Was this a case for Martha Rees to observe? Was this a time when Martha *Rees* should hang around outside a school and see what was going on?

It was always a temptation with her.

But a coroner's work is a strict job, which walks along narrow alleyways dictated by the government. They enquire – no more than that – into who has died, when they died and how they met their death. It is not a complicated remit though to the surviving family it is an important one. But sometimes – only sometimes – it is not enough. It does not really *explain* a death. Sequences of events lead up to untimely deaths. Not nature but something within the victim's life or even in the perpetrator's. The two lives collide. And mayhem results. It was her job to unravel the truth. And sometimes being a coroner, sitting behind a desk, does not colour in the picture enough to hold a satisfactory inquest.

Martha sat still for only a minute before making up her mind. She wanted not the black and white picture but the full Technicolor effect. And that would not come from sitting here. She stood up.

The door opened.

Jericho with a huge bunch of long stemmed, red roses.

She stared at him. Completely confused.

'These just arrived,' he said. 'By van.'

There is something about red roses. They mean love and romance. Or gratitude. But they always mean *something*. They never mean *nothing*. She took the flowers from him, only aware of a dry, sour taste in her mouth. She had done nothing to deserve these roses. She did not know who would send her red roses when it wasn't her birthday. She knew that these beautiful blooms did not mean love or gratitude. They were not emblems of a birthday or anniversary. They were reminders.

'There's a card with them. Open it.'

Jericho had a soft voice with a Shropshire burr which was spurring her on. She took the white envelope in her fingers.

Martha Gunn. That was all. Martha Gunn. *Her* name. The flowers were meant for *her*.

She opened the envelope, pulled out the white card.

These are for you, it read in the florist's hand. *This is your message, Martha.*

She stared at it and knew an old friend was back.

Last year she had been sent messages, records, small, tiny clues, hints that someone was trying to communicate with her. But like a Martian landing or a deaf and dumb person signing to her, Martha could not understand it.

She picked up the telephone.

This had gone far enough.

CHAPTER ELEVEN

Alex listened to her confused ramblings for a full ten minutes without interrupting. He heard about the scratched record which had been left at her door, the strange, intrusive whispering, the bunches of flowers – even the dead animals abandoned on the doorstep which she had initially blamed on Bobby – until Mark Sullivan had pointed out the ligature tied tightly round the mouse's neck. She tried to leave out all the 'weird feelings' before realising that this was a part of it too. She was not an imaginative woman.

Alex sat, concentrating hard, his entire body still, his fingers interwoven, his thin face set in a deep frown. 'I don't like the sound of this at all.'

'You take it seriously then?'

He nodded then tried to lighten his tone, the contradiction still making his eyes heavy and anxious.

'Not got a secret admirer, Martha?'

She tried to laugh. 'No.'

'I'm sure you have.'

'Alex,' she appealed. 'I don't want chivalry from you. I'm consulting you as a policeman. I'm worried. Truly I'm worried. Someone is sending me messages that I can't read. I don't know what they're saying or why they're saying it. I don't understand but it feels like a threat. My job brings me into contact with all sorts of strange people undergoing what can be a very stressful experience. I don't like mysteries, Alex. I live alone, in a relatively isolated house with my daughter and an au pair who is about to leave. Help me. Please.'

'I'll make some enquiries. Is that OK?'

'Yes. Please. Thank you.'

As he left he put an awkward hand on her shoulder. 'Think back into your past, Martha. The clue will be there somewhere. Consider anyone you've had bad dealings with. Especially if they appeared strange. If you do have any ideas who this might be get back to me. All right?'

'Yes.'

She felt happier having off-loaded her problem but still fidgety and tense. She sat and pondered over her past cases. There had been tragedy aplenty. Drownings and murders, terrible accidents and suffering. She had seen relatives scream at the verdict or cry or simply sit in the inquest, frozen in their seats. And then there were the suicides. Which brought her straight back to her most recent case, the deaths of the two teenagers. She felt she wanted to do something herself to set the record straight. It is, after all, she argued to herself, part of the duty of a coroner.

It was three o'clock in the afternoon. Schools came out at four. If she hurried home she could change and be outside the school gates as the children came out. Maybe there she could pick up on something.

On her way out she thrust the flowers at a startled Jericho. 'Here,' she said. 'Take these home for Mrs Palfreyman.'

He looked astonished and pushed them away from him as

though they scalded him. 'I can't do that. She'll think I'm having an extramarital.'

'Give them to her anyway.'

'She'll be very suspicious,' he said. 'Don't you like flowers?'

'Allergies,' she replied, and as she backed the car out of the drive she thought what a stupid thing to say that had been. She almost *always* had flowers on her desk. Roses, freesias, daffodils, hyacinths – depending on the season. But she found the sight of the long-stemmed, expensive roses threatening. She knew full well what they were a warning. A beacon. A lighthouse luring her towards rocks. Beautiful as they were they were alerting her to the fact that *he* was out there, with her in his sights. She couldn't have taken them home for them to invade her private life. And neither did she want them insinuating their not-so-subtle message from her desk.

No – let Mrs Palfreyman have the pleasure of them.

She smiled to herself. Jericho would soon talk his way out of any suspicion. She had never met a more inventive man when it came to stories. Many was the time she'd listened to him relating some incident and hardly recognised it for the embellishment.

She was home in less than fifteen minutes and changed into her blonde wig, big shades, dark tan make-up and a slash of vivid lipstick. Faded jeans, cowboy boots and a brown leather jacket completed the picture. She grinned at herself in the mirror and reflected how easy it was for a woman to alter her appearance completely.

No one would have known her.

She parked a little way from the school and wandered slowly towards it. One or two youngsters were already trickling through the gates – a little early.

She picked Katie Ashbourne out easily. Partly because the papers had been filled with pictures of her, partly because she was tall and also because of the cluster of admirers surrounding her. She had waist-length straight, brown hair. Her school skirt was halfway up her thighs and she had a rucksack tucked underneath her arm.

The girl gave Martha a cool, arrogant stare. Martha smiled back at her.

'You Press?' the girl asked.

'No. Why?'

'Oh.' The girl looked crestfallen; but she soon recovered. 'Only that I've been plagued by them.' She tossed her hair and tilted her face upwards, nose in the air. 'My boyfriend got murdered, see. The Press have been hounding me. In fact they've offered me thousands to tell my story but I don't know. Is it right? Is it wrong? Why shouldn't I anyway? I'm going to need money some day and the story'll pass, like any other.'

She was a child of her time. Streetwise, cool, confident and well read in the ways of her world.

Martha shed her coroner prejudices to assume the persona of Martha Rees, swaggering private eye. 'Exactly. I agree. Mind you – I'd be careful what I say to the Press – or even to anyone.' Even her voice sounded different, cocky and brash with a nasal Thames twang.

'Dead people can't sue.' The girl tossed her lovely hair away from her face again. The movement rippled it down her back.

She had wary dark eyes and an olive complexion and was more than averagely attractive. Martha wondered if she and

Gough would have stuck together. She doubted it.

'I suppose you're Katie Ashbourne then, are you?'

The girl chewed some gum which must have been parked in the side of her cheek. 'Yeah. It was my boyfriend who was killed. Roger Gough. DreadNought, we all called him.'

Martha adjusted her shades to peep over them. 'Really?'

'Yeah. Dead nice bloke. Killed by a psycho, he was. Funny thing is we never realised Hughes was a psycho. Roger weren't frightened of him none. But then – that were Roger. Brave.'

'Didn't you realise that the Hughes boy was a psycho?'

'Nah. But they're good at hidin' it, aren't they, psychos?'

Martha Rees shrugged. 'Why did Hughes pick on your boyfriend? Was it over you?'

'Not exactly. Well.' The hair rippled down her back again. 'Sort of. There was always a bit of trouble between Wilfred and DreadNought.'

Martha frowned. 'Wilfred?'

'After Wilfred Owen, the poet. That's what we used to call him on account of him likin' poetry and stuff.'

'Oh. I didn't know.'

'Well he did. Used to sit and read the stuff. Anyway,' she tossed her head again and took a long open-mouthed chew at her gum, 'Hughes had a sort of thing about me. Used to fancy me somethin' rotten. He flashed at me once,' she said defiantly. 'And DreadNought. Well, let's just say he didn't like other people goin' for me. But DreadNought was safe.' She smiled. 'I didn't fancy the little bleeder. I wouldn't have gone off with him.' She grinned. 'If there'd been me and Wilfred on a desert island surrounded by a shark-infested sea I'd have swum. That's what I thought of him. He was a creep.'

Martha nodded and grimaced back. The description was graphic enough to paint the picture of a lonely, isolated boy picked on by his schoolmates, ridiculed for all that he found interesting. The portrait depressed her.

She turned around to scan the crowd of children streaming out of the school gates. 'Which one is Chelsea Arnold?'

Katie Ashbourne didn't like the attention shifting away from her. 'You don't want to speak to her.'

Martha lowered her shades back over her eyes. She knew it gave her a mysterious look and Katie Ashbourne fell for it. 'Oh. Well, that's her,' she said, pointing towards a small girl scurrying out of the side gate.

Martha walked along the pavement, turning in and bumping into the girl. 'Oh, I'm sorry,' she said. 'Goodness.' Even she was impressed by the surprise she managed to inject into her tone. 'It's Chelsea, isn't it?'

The girl looked up and Martha had an impression of a twitching, brown-eyed, little mouse.

'Surely you know me, Chelsea? I'm a friend of your mother's dear.'

Martha was taking a gamble. If there is anyone a teenage girl does not remember it is the friends of her mother's. The women her mother drones on and on about whose names and faces all blur into one.

The girl fell for it. 'Oh yes,' she lied. 'I remember you.'

Martha took another gamble. 'We're the ones who went to live in Spain, dear.'

Chelsea Arnold's face cleared and Martha knew she had struck lucky.

'I'm sure I read about you in the paper the other day,' Martha continued. 'Weren't you saying something about – now what was it? Oh yes. There was some trouble at the school, wasn't there? Didn't a friend of yours get hurt?'

Chelsea looked around her but there was no one within earshot. 'Yes,' she said. 'A friend of mine died. He was stabbed and he died in hospital.'

'Was he a close friend, dear?'

Chelsea nodded but no pain crossed her face.

'And what about the boy who did it?'

This time the girl looked truly upset. 'He killed himself,' she said quietly, 'in Stoke Heath.'

So Martha had her answer. 'Dear, dear,' she said. 'How awful. And was he a friend of yours too?'

The girl looked at her, tears making her eyes very bright.

Martha plunged on. 'And didn't your mother say something about an accident? Your wrist – wasn't it?'

The girl stared at her, round-eyed. Then without a word she turned and scuttled off.

Martha watched her go feeling sorry for her. She was very young to have had such tragedy so very near her. And now she was being forced to toe the party line or she would be ostracised.

We are judged by the people we mix with.

In the car she removed the blonde wig, ruffled up her own hair and smiled at herself in the mirror. It had been a successful foray.

But she was still missing something.

She decided to call in Simon Boyd's on the way home. The transformation of Martin's study was just beginning to take shape and colour in her mind. The walls painted with satin ivory emulsion and the windows hung with the same coloured curtains decorated with the darkest of huge red flowers. She was starting to see it. She would have the floorboards cleaned and sanded, buy some new furniture. She was looking over the bolts of material when she suddenly felt unaccountably disloyal and instead of seeing the rolls of material she saw Martin's face, looking at her and seeming unbearably sad.

She left the shop and drove home, her mind in turmoil.

CHAPTER TWELVE

At seven-thirty that evening, just as she was putting a chicken Caesar salad on the table, she heard a knock at the door and opened it to Alex Randall. 'What a brilliant surprise,' she said

He hesitated. 'Sorry for coming unannounced,' he said, looking oddly bashful. 'But I was passing and...'

'Come in,' she said. 'No – don't worry, I love it when people drop by. Are you hungry by any chance? I'm just about to put tea on the table.'

'Yes. It so happens I am. Ravenous.'

'Then I'm glad I made a bit extra.'

He followed her into the kitchen where Agnetha and Sukey were already tucking in. Martha fished out another knife and fork from the drawer, introduced Alex to her daughter and the au pair who at least did stop eating for a second to say hello. Unlike Sukey.

'Tuck in,' Martha invited, handing him a plate and the bowl. 'Truth is I haven't really got used to Sam's not being here and I invariably cook too much.'

'His loss is my gain,' he said. 'Caesar salad's my favourite. Particularly when it has both chicken and bacon in it and a nice, strong sauce.'

'Mine too.'

'Yeah,' Sukey said grumpily. 'We have it about twice a week.'

Alex turned towards her. 'So what's your favourite then?'

'Lasagne with salad,' Sukey said firmly.

'And yours, Agnetha?'

'I think poached salmon,' Agnetha said. 'The wild ones not the farmed ones.'

'Can you taste the difference?'

'Of course, Mr Randall.'

'Hmm,' he said dubiously.

They spent the meal eating voraciously (Alex had told the truth when he had claimed to be ravenous) and ragging each other good-humouredly. As soon as they had finished Martha left Agnetha and Sukey to fill the dishwasher and led Alex into Martin's study. She didn't want them hearing what he might have to say.

Alex settled down in the upholstered leather library chair. 'This is comfortable,' he said. 'A real man's chair.'

Martha nodded. 'It was Martin's favourite.' She waited for the familiar stab of pain but this evening it did not come. She waited but it was gone. A memory only.

'Would you like a whisky or something?'

He sighed. 'Better not. I'm driving. Set a good example. Anyway I thought you'd want to know where I've got to with my investigations. The two prison officers are both on their days off,' he said. 'Back tomorrow. I thought I'd call round first thing in the morning. I could pop over to your office at lunchtime and let you know what they said.' He looked around the room. 'Was this Martin's study?'

She nodded. 'Sukey and I are going to revamp it,' she said. 'It's

a much nicer room than my study which is an old dressing room
– almost a corridor and a bit dark. This overlooks the garden
and is really lovely all the year round. There are views out the
back, straight into the woods. We're going to do the whole lot,
new furniture, new curtains, strip the walls, sand the floors.'

'You're moving on?'

She nodded. 'It's time, Alex. We all need to move on.
Agnetha, Sukey, Sam and me too.'

'So,' he said, smiling. 'That's good. That's what people
should do in life. Move on. If they can.' Something crossed his
face and she thought to herself what an enigma he was. She
knew so little about him. Almost nothing.

'Now to the other business. The flowers. We've made
enquiries at the florist's. They're from a woman, Martha.'

'A woman?' She couldn't have been more astonished.

'Yes. A woman. She paid in cash.' His face broke into a
smile. 'You can take some consolation from the fact that you
don't come cheap. They cost forty five-pounds.'

She felt a snigger. 'And now Mrs Palfreyman has them and
according to Jericho is going to suspect him of having an
extramarital.' She mimicked Jericho's Shropshire burr.

They both chuckled for a moment. Then Martha asked a
leading question. 'Did the florist give a description of her?'

'Yes. Young, late twenties, early thirties, brown hair, slim
build, pale complexion. Dressed in combat trousers and an
olive green beaded jacket. Nicely spoken. No regional accent
and the girl didn't know her. Does it fit the description of
anyone you know?'

Martha shook her head. 'I can't think of anyone specific.
Which shop was it?'

'The florist's at Harlescott. The one opposite the bus station.'

Martha knew the place. It was avant-garde, fashionable, selling twigs and orange bulrushes, long blue feathery plants and terracotta pots. She'd ordered bouquets from there herself, tempted by the buckets of blooms which always stood outside, on the pavement, which was a convenient pull off point being wide enough for parking.

'I don't understand,' she said. 'I simply don't understand. The hints and suggestions must be all connected. The message is always the same – message for Martha.' She could feel her face freeze. 'It didn't feel like a threat from a woman.'

'Well there's no law against sending flowers, you know. Perhaps you're reading too much into it.'

'But the other things, Alex?'

'It wouldn't count as stalking until they've crossed the line into intrusion.

'It's a matter of degree and it has to get quite oppressive before you can take out an injunction against them. The whole thing would be very public. And the idea of a threat coming from a woman would make you seem—'

She could imagine. 'Either a dyke or a wimp who couldn't cope with a bit of attention from a small, young, gentle female. She wouldn't be perceived as a threat. And I'd get no sympathy.'

'Exactly.'

'So that's why you wanted to come here rather than in the office where Jericho's ear seems to pick everything up.'

Again he nodded, his eyes fixed on hers and she felt helpless. 'But the voices I heard. It wasn't a woman. It just wasn't. I know.'

'But Martha, the flowers came from a woman. This seems a gentle, female message rather than overt, physical threats.'

'But it is someone who bears a grudge against me?'

'I don't know. No – more like someone wanting you to see things from their point of view.'

'But how can I when I can't understand what it is that they're trying to say?'

'Wait,' he said. 'It'll become bolder. In the end they will expose themselves. Otherwise there is no point to it.'

She exploded into laughter. 'Well that I don't relish, a young woman exposing herself.'

He laughed with her again. 'I will ask the bobbies on the beat to keep an eye on the florist's shop but if she's any subtlety about her she won't go there again but to one of the other florist's. And that's assuming she pursues the flowers theme. Next time it might be something else.'

Like a noose around a dead mouse's neck?

Alex stood up and put a friendly hand on her shoulder. 'Wait and see. That's my advice. I don't think you're in any danger.'

And that, Martha thought, was the traditional trick of the stalker, to appear innocuous. They appear so right up until they are ready to strike.

Alex was as good as his word. The following morning, a little after eleven, he called round to Martha's office with transcripts of the two prison officers' statements.

Walton Pembroke's first.

'Callum Hughes arrived at Stoke Heath at a little after ten o'clock in the evening of the 6th of September. He seemed quiet, a bit frightened, not aggressive. Doctor Delyth Fontaine

had seen him the evening before and pronounced him fit for detention. He'd been allocated cell 101 and seemed a bit nervous of his cellmate. We introduced them.'

Martha rejected the silly vision of a formal introduction, 'Tyrone, this is...' followed by a public school shaking of hands. More like the back treatment and a couple of grunts. Maybe, when the screws had left, a bit of eyeballing. And then the vicious kick to show Callum Hughes what he could expect if he did not toe the Tyrone-line.

She continued reading. *'When we called in a few hours later, at eleven o'clock, he was a bit panicky and we allowed him out to walk along the passageway to reassure him. We took him back to his cell about ten minutes later. When we called in at twelve he was fast asleep, like a baby, and we left him. At six-thirty a.m. the next morning his cellmate pushed the panic button and we found him hanging. He'd used some computer wire and looped it round the side of the bed. We cut him down but he was well dead.'*

There was nothing there. Martha met Alex's eyes. Silently he handed her the other statement.

She started reading.

'Callum Hughes arrived at Stoke Heath at a little after ten o'clock...'

In essence it was identical. Practically word for word.

Alex Randall was watching her, chewing his lip.

'Well,' she said, 'this is a coincidence. At least no one can accuse them of telling different stories. Their perception of events that night correspond. Better than most witness statements.'

Silently he nodded, his dark eyes watching her with that

same faintly worried frown and she knew he was not one hundred per cent happy about this either. She tried to flush him out.

'Do we suspect collusion?'

'Could be,' he said cautiously.

'Did you talk to Tyrone Smith again?'

'I did.'

'And?'

'And nothing. He didn't give anything more away.'

'There's something here,' she said, her eyes drifting across the sheets of paper. 'There's something wrong.'

'Are you playing policeman again, Martha?'

'Could be,' she said, equally cautiously. 'Oh, come on, Alex,' she appealed. 'There *is* something odd here. For a start we have no satisfactory explanation of the bruising either on Callum's chest or on his face.'

He lifted his eyebrows.

'Something's not right,' she said, picking up the phone. 'I'm going to talk to Mark again. I'm not happy, Alex. And until I feel we've reached the truth I will not release Callum's body for burial.'

'Well that's your prerogative,' he said. 'But I hope you're sure.'

This time it was she who queried his words. 'Well, what I mean is, all along you've had some sympathy with this boy.'

'I see him as a victim.'

'But I don't,' he said. 'I see him as a—'

She supplied the word. 'Psycho?'

'No,' he said slowly, 'not that but in the end he was a

killer and DreadNought was the victim. Hughes might have been a frightened youngster who lashed out through fright but in the end he was still a killer. Talk to Mark,' he said, 'by all means but I don't think he'll take you any further on in your quest. The boy was a killer. He struck a fatal wound. And in the end, even if Gough was a bully, he didn't deserve that.'

'No. I agree.'

'Good.' Randall smiled. 'So at least we agree on something.'

She felt her face relax. 'Of course,' she said. 'I think that in this case it's simply that our perspectives lie in slightly different directions.' She stood up. 'And Alex, by the way, thank you for enquiring about the flowers. I do appreciate it.'

'You feel better now?'

She nodded. 'Much.'

She might feel better, she reflected, as she closed the door behind him, but she was twice as puzzled.

When Alex Randall had gone she picked up the telephone, reached Mark Sullivan's voicemail and left a message asking him to telephone her office first thing in the morning. As she did so she crossed her fingers that for once he would be stone-cold sober to consider her questions in his best, most intelligent, most dispassionate, pathologist's mind.

But Martha was not one to lie and wait, bleating like a tethered goat at the foot of a tree. Before she went to work on the following day she arranged for electric gates to be installed at the bottom of the drive and CCTV cameras to cover both front and back of the house. She rang the burglar alarm company and asked them to come early to service the system. At the same time she rang and asked the farmer to check on all the fences.

This done, she felt a measure more secure.

And now she felt a prisoner in her own home.

CHAPTER THIRTEEN

She was at her desk a little after half past eight in the morning having spent a sleepless night, filled with uncomfortable dreams of boys fighting. For some reason she was imagining it all ways, simple schoolboy scuffles, young soldiers at war, boys on the football pitch. Sam, Callum, Roger Gough all morphing into one surprisingly threatening boy. At three a.m. she got up, made herself a cup of decaffeinated coffee and went back to bed to drink it, knees hunched up, a dressing gown over her shoulders. Something was bothering her, sneaking up from behind and then hiding when she turned so she couldn't see it clearly – only the very hint of a glimpse of a shadow, some moving light which vanished when she tried to see it more clearly. Something was not right. But she didn't have a clue what it was. And she was worried about Sam. He had seemed different when she'd seen him, distant and in her heart she knew he had moved on, without her mother's circle.

She finally dropped off to sleep for what seemed like seconds and awoke to a cool, grey morning, damp with the moisture of autumn, and a thick mist which hung lazily over the ground, shrouding grass and driveway alike so the trees looked as though their trunks vanished into cotton wool.

It seemed an uninspiring morning. But one wish, at least,

was granted. At a quarter past nine her phone rang and Jericho put a breezy and sober Mark Sullivan through.

'Martha. Morning. I got your message. What can I do for you?'

'Mark, you'll have to help me here. It's about the Callum Hughes case.'

'Thought it might be,' he said, suddenly testy and guarded.

'Alex has re-interviewed the two prison officers who were on duty the night he died.'

'Yes?'

'Their statements are identical – word for word. Suspicious in itself.'

'Depends on your index of mistrust. Maybe that is what actually happened.'

She ignored the hint. 'There's no mention of any sort of fracas that would explain the bruising on Callum's shoulder and the back of his chest. I'm really not happy to release the body for burial, Mark. The boy was young, vulnerable and in custody. He'd never made a suicide attempt before. The custodial system is therefore responsible and we have a duty to make sure that justice has been done. His mother wants a full enquiry. Can you help me here, Mark? Do you have any ideas how the bruising might have occurred?'

'You've an explanation for the shin injury? That was the true assault. The others were just minor bangs.'

'Oh yes. Callum's little cell mate decided he'd put one on him – more or less to teach the critter a lesson as far as I can gather.'

Mark Sullivan gave a barely audible groan. 'I guess that happens plenty along the line. But Martha I can't always think up an explanation for bruising on a body, particularly when I can't be absolutely sure whether they were inflicted just before or even just after death occurred. He might have banged into the side of the bed as he was hanging or swung around in a death throe. All I can say, Martha, with certainty, is that this bruising was minor. It did not cause his death. He simply stopped breathing, due to the ligature round his neck. There were clear marks of asphyxiation. You saw the post-mortem findings yourself. The distribution of the lividity was exactly as I would have anticipated; the congestion and sub pleural petechiae in the brain and other major organs are also wholly consistent. There's nothing that puts any doubt in my mind that this was death by a suicidal hanging.'

'You misunderstand me, Mark. I'm not questioning the mode of Callum's death. I merely want some explanation of the bruising – apart from that around the neck.'

Sullivan gave a doubtful, 'Hmm. I don't have your need for such detailed explanations,' he said. 'As far as I'm concerned the bruises were caused by something blunt and probably happened a little while before his death so it could be anything. Even your little friend, Tyrone.'

'I can't think why he would have confessed to a more serious injury and deny a couple of thumps.'

'Perhaps his feeble brain thought if he confessed to two assaults it would indicate a more sustained attack which in turn might have been the key that unlocked Callum Hughes's suicide-wish which would have implicated Tyrone Smith even further. He might even have thought it could lead to a charge. It's even possible he could have shoved Hughes hard and not even considered it an assault so felt he had nothing to confess to. Come on, Martha', he said, suddenly impatient, 'you know what these young thugs are like. Illogical to say the least.'

'Yes.'

But according to everyone, even to Smith, he had been knocked out by his sleeping tablet.

This time it was Martha who wanted to groan. How could you progress with a case when you believed everyone could be lying?

The prison officers?

Both of them?

One covering for the other?

She couldn't rule it out. Her instinct was that between them Pembroke and Stevie Matthews had roughed the boy up – just a little. And if that were so she would say something when she wound up the inquest. Something about a culture of bullying inevitably leading to tragedy. It would be expected that she would make some comment about better supervision for young offenders.

She ended the conversation with the pathologist and put the phone down.

There was something else that seemed untidy when she would have preferred something a bit neater.

Although Shelley Hughes and her son had been close, the boy had ended his life without leaving any sort of note to her. There had been no final farewell to his mother. No reassurance that he was all right.

There is no danger down here, or if any, it will be well over before you read these lines.'

* * *

She found it hard to work that morning.

It was the morning she had set aside to fill in her annual audit figures for the National Statistics, a chore that she usually found interesting, looking at the epidemiology of disease throughout North Shropshire and comparing it with other parts of the country.

She worked for an hour or more, accepted a coffee from Jericho and bent her head back over the figures.

It made grim reading. She sighed, sat back from her desk, glanced at her watch. It was still only twelve o'clock and she'd finished her morning's work. And now she felt restless and fidgety. She needed to do something. On impulse she lifted her mobile phone from her bag and dialled her best friend's number.

'Miranda,' she said when it was answered. 'What are you doing for lunch?'

Her friend's voice was muffled and she could hear traffic in the background.

'Just going into the hairdresser's, my dear, but I'll be free in an hour. And in answer to your question nothing and I'm already starving.'

They arranged to meet at one at The Peach Tree, a modernistic restaurant opposite the old Abbey, which served the best lunches in Shrewsbury.

She still had an hour to kill, so she turned her attention to the revamp of Martin's room. He had had an eye for good, antique furniture and in his study there was a walnut secretaire, early Victorian, full of leather bound legal books, which Martin had treasured. She'd decided to keep the books in case either Sam or Sukey wanted to head for the Bar but she didn't want the furniture. She'd never liked it. The trouble was it was probably worth quite a bit of money. Martin had acquired it soon after they'd bought their first house, at a country house sale in Gloucestershire and it was heavy and very good quality. In the room was also a pair of leather upholstered library chairs, early nineteenth century, which were also worth something and a William IV rosewood library table which she'd also never liked, quite unfairly, on account of it having bulbous legs.

Martha had considered putting them in the local saleroom but when she had made enquiries she had learned that on top of the purchase price there was a buyer's premium, which held values down. Perhaps, she thought, it would be easier if she invited a local dealer round to value them. Then, if the price was right, she could sell them to him and he could transport them away.

It seemed too easy a solution.

She parked outside the Abbey, walked past Gay Meadow, sad now that the football ground, which had been in the same place since 1910, was to move. There was something exciting about having it on the edge of the town; it involved all the townsfolk. She wondered if the atmosphere would be lost when the football ground was more remote. She smiled at a recollection an old man had told her. In its early days the football ground had not been enclosed and the River Severn, being nearby, received many a ball. So Fred Davies, in his coracle, was entrusted with its retrieval and the resumption of the game. Wisely a fence was finally erected around it and the game was no longer halted by Fred's slow paddle in his coracle. It might have been sensible but from then something of the essence of this old town's history was lost for ever. The river had its naughty side too, flooding the pitch whenever it rose and putting paid to any match. Perhaps it was better the ground was moved.

She crossed the English Bridge and started to walk up Wyle Cop. Just before she reached the Period House Shop she peered through the window into the small antiques shop she'd first noticed a year ago. As she'd hoped Finton Cley was in there, on his own, sitting on a settle, smoking what looked like a Sherlock Holmes meerschaum pipe. She pushed the door open. He grinned at her, unsurprised.

'Martha Gunn,' he said, in a mocking tone. 'What can I do for you?'

'I think I might have some stuff to sell.'

'Think?' he queried, 'Stuff? What does it depend on and what is it?'

'I'm redecorating my husband's study. I have a few pieces.'

'Ye-es?' He blew out a waft of smoke.

'A library table.'

'Wood?' he asked without taking the pipe out of his mouth.

'I think it's rosewood. Probably William the Fourth.'

'Know how much you want for it?'

'I've an idea,' she said.

'Anything else?'

'A double-heighted secretaire. Walnut. Victorian, with a glazed front. The leather inside is original and in nice condition. I don't think it was used much as a secretaire.'

'They never were,' he mumbled, removing the pipe from his mouth now and studying it closely before putting it back in his mouth. 'Awkward things. They don't look right closed and there's something clumsy about them open. The drawer looks too big. Mistake of a piece, I always think. Still. Always worth a look. Anything else, Martha Gunn?'

Why did he always smile when he spoke her name? As though he knew something that she did not. It intrigued her and annoyed her in equal quantities.

She'd deliberately saved the best till last. 'Two leather upholstered armchairs. I'm pretty sure they're earlier. Regency. Chippendale – or at least one of his disciples. I think they're what you call Cuban mahogany. They're very heavy and on brass casters and the wood is dark with a distinctive shade of red.'

He gave out a whistle. ' Mmm,' he said. 'They sound nice. When can I take a look?'

'Whenever.'

'Tomorrow evening?'

'Fine.'

She gave him directions to the White House and he promised to come at six.

She just had time to nip up to Appleyards and buy some olives stuffed with garlic to set out before supper. And then was tempted by a display of French cheeses which reminded her of long ago camping holidays with Martin and the then tiny twins, picnics of French sticks and cheese with tomatoes followed by *pain au chocolat* which they had devoured greedily, leaving only crumbs in the grass. She gave a sudden smile at the thought of Martin, hiking, with one twin on his back, knowing she was a mirror image.

She walked quickly back down Wyle Cop with its precarious-looking black and white Tudor buildings, Henry

Tudor House – where Henry VII had stayed the night before his fight with Richard III at Bosworth field – and the Lion Hotel, Shrewsbury's old coaching inn. In such an ancient town it is impossible not to feel that every step you take you are treading on history.

Miranda was already seated when she arrived at The Peach Tree. It looked bright and pretty in the autumn sunshine and she had chosen a seat right in the window, overlooking the Abbey, still with its ragged wall marking the spot where the cloisters had been – until Henry VIII had sacked the monasteries, dispersed the monks and demolished their quarters.

Miranda's hair was looking immaculate which reminded Martha it was time she ran the gauntlet of another visit to her hairdresser, Vernon Grubb. Miranda had glossy, blonde hair which she had always worn in a Sixties bob, just reaching the chin. It had gone in and out of fashion but wisely Miranda had never altered it: not colour (suspiciously), not length, not style, always with a swept aside half-fringe. It suited her. Martha could not imagine her with any other hairstyle. Sometimes she tried – and gave up.

Her friend half-rose and kissed her cheek. Miranda had been a medical student friend of hers, had attended her wedding – as she had attended hers. They had been close for what seemed like for ever. Miranda had worked in Public Health, had two children, seemed idyllically happy married to Steven. And then a year ago, at the age of thirty-five, she had found herself pregnant again. Through the Alpha Feta protein test it had been discovered that the child had Down's syndrome. And then slowly, Miranda's seemingly enviable and perfect life had begun to unravel. She and Steven had quarrelled bitterly. She had wanted a termination while he had objected, not even through religious belief and, privately, Martha had thought it was simply that he disbelieved the evidence. He could not accept that any child of his could possibly carry a defect. The rest, as they say, was history. Miranda had had the termination, Steven had left her and, embittered, had tried to brainwash the two children that their mother had murdered their baby sister. It had been a cruel thing to do and looking at her friend's face Martha thought that she seemed to look older than her thirty-six years in spite of the slim figure, the tight jeans, black high-heeled leather boots, skilful make-up and glamorous hair. The artistic clothes had the effect of drawing attention to her friend's strain.

'Well,' Miranda said, 'so how *are* you?' She opened her blue eyes wide.

'Gosh,' she said. 'You look well. Really well. Better than I've seen you look for ages. So tell me your secret. What's going on in *your* life?'

Martha started laughing. 'Enough.'

'A little bird told me you'd been wined and dined by a certain businessman?'

'I suppose you're talking about Simon Pendlebury.'

'I suppose I am,' Miranda said coyly. 'Well?'

'How the hell do you know?'

'A friend of mine was in the restaurant that night.'

'Yes, we've had dinner. We're friends. Why not?'

'No reason why not,' Miranda said. 'Except I wouldn't have thought he was your type.'

'No – I'm not sure he's my type either. But we enjoy each other's company.'

'I'm intrigued. So?'

'So nothing, 'Martha said, laughing. 'We have dinner sometimes. That's it. Period. End of story.'

'Well – he's a widower and you're alone too.'

Martha was glad Miranda hadn't said the word, widow. She hated it. It sounded so hopeless, as though nothing was on the horizon, as though she was squeezed dry of all romance.

'We do enjoy each other's company,' Martha said. 'But as for love – marriage. Come on,' she said. 'It's a big thing second time around. I have Sukey and Sam. And I'm not a young girl any more. I'm older – more cynical. More guarded, I suppose. I'm not sure.'

'Experience,' Miranda said, almost shuddering.

The waiter took their order, red onion tart for Martha, sausage and mash for Miranda.

'So what's Steven been up to now?'

'Oh – the usual mind games. Not bringing the children back when they're due, sitting, watching me from his car when I leave for work, sending me bunches of dead flowers. Honestly, Martha. I don't think he's right in the head. Something about that – business – has damaged him. I can't recognise him for who he was. Sometimes he even frightens me.'

'Seriously?'

'Do you think he blames me for all the business?'

'He blames the entire medical profession, Martha. He holds them personally responsible for what happened.'

Miranda nodded, glanced out of the window. 'Oh no,' she said.

Steven was a thin, bespectacled man. He'd always been pale but the face pressed against the window was bone-white. Even Martha shrank away from him. He bared his teeth at her, mouthed something then turned away leaving her wondering. Was he her secret stalker?

Miranda turned back into the restaurant. 'He's always there,' she said simply.

'Doesn't he go to work?'

'I think he's off sick,' Miranda said. 'He'd be better if he did go to work. Give him something else to think about. As it is, he hasn't moved on.' Her face looked weary.

Martha decided it would be cruel to tell her about her stalker. She sneaked another glance out of the window. Steven Mountford had vanished.

'So what are you up to,' Miranda asked brightly.

'The schoolboy suicide and murder.'

'Oh, that nasty stabbing in the school. And in Shrewsbury too.' Miranda was affronted. 'So the boy committed suicide in remorse?'

'I don't know,' Martha said. And in her voice she could hear creeping doubt.

They talked some more but they both knew that their lunch had been soured – as no doubt Steven Mountford had meant it to be.

They ordered coffees, tried to avoid looking in the direction of the window and their conversation dried up while Miranda looked more and more abstracted.

Martha drove back to the office in thoughtful mood.

It didn't help that Roger Gough's inquest was looming and she expected trouble – some sort of outburst from his parents. It would be yet another set of headlines for Shelley Hughes to endure.

CHAPTER FOURTEEN

Martha usually set some time aside before an inquest to speak to the relatives and try and prepare them for what lay ahead but the Goughs arrived late, and she had the feeling that it was deliberate.

Christina had had a black T-shirt printed with a picture of her son as though he was a Catholic saint or a pop star. It sat on her plump figure, the boy's face distorted over her ample bosom, his eyes very dark and staring but the plump cheeks making it easy to identify him. Underneath Roger Gough's face was his name and the date of his birth and death. *15th March 1992 – 16th September 2005*. It had been a short life.

Dramatically underneath that was a blood-stained knife and a single word: '*Murdered*'.

Today Christina was wearing an ankle-length black gypsy skirt with a wide, leather belt slung around her plump hips, high-heeled boots and huge, jangling earrings. She stood in front of Martha, staring hard, breathing heavily. Then she dropped heavily into the seat Jericho showed her. Martha acknowledged her with a nod. She knew instinctively that a smile would be misinterpreted as improper levity on her part.

At Christina's side, her husband was more soberly dressed, in a dark suit, white shirt and black tie. He didn't look at

Martha as he sat down but alternated his stares between the floor and his wife's profile, his eyes sliding up in an arc between the two.

Martha gave an inward groan as the Press filed in at the back. Five of them. Two were cub reporters from the *Shropshire Star* and the *Shrewsbury Chronicle* and would be no problem. She knew their style – to report without fanning the flames. But there were another three who were unfamiliar. At a guess the skinny girl with the sharp features, flicking her ponytail behind her, was from a tabloid. She would almost certainly already have taken a preliminary statement from the parents of the dead boy and that was why Mr and Mrs Gough had entered the courtroom late. To add to Martha's concern, just as she was about to open the inquest, she saw Shelley Hughes scuttle to the very back of the room, her head bent, as though to avoid being recognised. Luckily neither the Goughs nor any of their party noticed her or there would have been a scene. And she appeared to have passed unrecognised by the Press.

Martha opened the inquest in the normal way, giving Roger Gough's name, the date and place of his death and immediately the trouble started.

Christina Gough stood up. 'Why don't you say,' she said savagely, 'what he was doing in the hospital in the first place?'

'We'll get to that,' Martha said calmly, 'in time. You'll have your chance to speak, Mrs Gough.'

It should have been enough. But Christina glared at Martha defiantly. 'I'm warning you. We don't want no cover up,' she said, jabbing her finger into the air towards her. 'We want what's right by our lad.'

Martha nodded. 'Absolutely,' she said. 'And that is what you will get. Now please – Mrs Gough do sit down. I do understand your distress but this must be done properly out of respect for your son. Your turn will come but first of all we need the police evidence.'

It was unfortunate, to have to relate the circumstances which had led to Roger Gough being hospitalised but a necessary step. Wherever her sympathies or desire for a balanced hearing lay Martha knew she could only return one verdict – homicide. And there was no doubt who was responsible. Rarely had a murder been witnessed by so many.

So it fell to Sergeant Paul Talith to step up to the witness box and take the oath to swear by Almighty God to tell the truth, the whole truth and nothing but the truth.

Like most police he used accepted police jargon.

'At four-thirty-five on September the sixth of this year Police Constable Gethin Roberts and myself were called to Hallow's Lane Comprehensive School where we had been told there had been a serious assault. The caller had told us an ambulance was also needed as a boy had been stabbed in the chest. We arrived at the same time as the ambulance crew who dealt with the boy who was seriously injured. We took statements from the witnesses and apprehended a class mate of the injured boy.' Talith gave Martha a swift glance.

'The boy who was injured was identified as Roger Gough. An officer accompanied him in the ambulance to the hospital while I called for assistance and accompanied the perpetrator to Monkmoor police station.'

'Thank you.'

A member of the ambulance crew was called next and

proved to be a young blonde woman in a dark uniform who identified herself as Janey Fryer, a qualified paramedic for five years.

She repeated much of what Paul Talith had said, adding her own contribution.

'We found the boy identified as Roger Gough lying on the ground. He was shocked and gasping for air but conscious.'

Martha stole a look at Christina Gough. She was ghost-pale, gripping her husband's hand, and staring at Janey Fryer, with her mouth slackly open.

'Roger Gough was bleeding from a chest wound just below his left nipple. We were unable to stabilise his condition. His blood pressure was dropping. We were unable to staunch the flow of blood. Under the circumstances we decided that the best thing to do was to advise the hospital we were on our way and administer intravenous fluids. We drove him at speed to the hospital using the siren and the blue light. PC Roberts sat in the back with him. On our arrival at the Royal Shrewsbury Hospital major injuries unit the doctors took responsibility for our patient. His condition was then critical. He was still losing blood and was barely conscious.'

Christina Gough wiped her eyes.

Martha dismissed the paramedic. 'Thank you.'

Next she called on the young doctor who had been working on the emergency surgical team the afternoon that Gough had been admitted.

She was a slim, young, Indian woman, dressed in a dark green sari. She had long, black hair, rolled in a neat bun on the nape of her neck and a red spot in the centre of her forehead. She gave her name as Sarinda Begum.

In a quiet voice she continued the story.

'At a quarter past five on Tuesday afternoon, September the 6th, I was bleeped and informed that a serious chest injury was expected, a stab wound. We prepared the theatre staff for emergency thoracic surgery. When Roger Gough, the patient, arrived, his blood pressure was unrecordable and he was still losing blood. He had a stab wound a little below the left nipple and a punctured lung. He was in a collapsed state, unconscious and unresponsive but breathing for himself at that point. We gave him oxygen and intravenous fluids. A chest x-ray showed he had a large pneumothorax, air in the lung, and we inserted a chest drain. His ecg was normal. We decided to try and stabilise his condition before deciding whether he needed chest surgery or not. By that evening it appeared that his condition *was* stabilising. His blood pressure, though still low, was recordable and the air on his chest was draining through an underwater seal. We had him on a ventilator. He was still a very sick boy but off the critical list.

'By the Wednesday Roger Gough looked as though he would recover but on x-ray the pneumothorax was not getting any smaller and we were concerned that air was still leaking in so we decided he needed surgery to repair the stab wound. It proved very difficult. The point of the knife had penetrated within millimetres of the heart and major blood vessels. We did the best we could but when he came out of the anaesthetic he was unable to breathe for himself and had to be ventilated. To keep a patient on a ventilator it is necessary to sedate them and sometimes this immobility can lead to a chest infection. This was the case with Roger Gough. In spite of prophylactic intravenous antibiotics he developed a severe chest infection and on the Thursday his condition was giving us concern. Ultimately he did not regain consciousness and on the Friday morning his condition deteriorated further. His heart could not cope and developed arrhythmias. On the Friday evening, following consultation with Roger's parents, the decision was taken to switch the ventilator off. The damage to Roger's major organs made life unsustainable. His parents sat with him. He was pronounced dead at six p.m. that evening.'

Her black eyes displayed no emotion even when they flickered over Roger Gough's parents. To Doctor Begum this was her job. She had done the best she could, been professional, taken the recognised steps, lost a patient. Not the first and in her job it would not be the last.

Martha picked up a movement at the back of the court. Faced with the consequences of her son's action Shelley Hughes was slipping away. Martha glanced at Gough's parents. They were sitting hand in hand, stone-still, too shocked to react.

It was time to take a break.

The Goughs were chastened when Jericho handed them some coffee and Rich Tea biscuits. They accepted them as though they were zombies, each action slow and automatic. Martha had seen this before. They would not have heard their son's death described in such graphic details. Christina Gough looked as though she had been punched in the solar plexus. Billy Gough spoke then. 'There's lots of his pals what want to speak up for him. That's allowed, isn't it?' His voice was truculent.

'Yes – within limits. Best to restrict it to one or two.'

Christina dabbed her eyes with a white handkerchief. It

came away blackened with mascara. 'He had loads of friends, our lad.'

'I'm sure.'

'That villain, on the other hand, had nobody.'

Martha felt compelled to speak. 'This is a double tragedy – for both sets of parents.'

Billy Gough snorted. 'Hughes started it.'

No he didn't, Martha thought. It was your *son who set in motion this trail of events.*

'I want you to say that,' Christina Gough said, her eyes fixed on Martha's face. 'I want you to *say* it. Say *something* about my lad being innocent and...'

'It wouldn't be appropriate,' Martha said. 'It isn't my place. I don't know why Callum Hughes set on your son.'

''Cos he were a psycho,' Billy Gough said grumpily.

'I've heard other coroners say things about people. Why won't you?'

'Not in this case,' Martha said firmly. 'I'm sorry. It wouldn't be appropriate.'

Billy Gough stared at her.'You've more sympathy for the little killer than our lad,' he said.

Martha took comfort in her usual role. 'It isn't my place to have sympathy, Mr Gough,' she said. 'I simply have a job to do.'

They both treated her to a long, hard stare and then filed out, muttering.

Mark Sullivan was next to give evidence.

He was factual, describing the state of the lungs, the course of the original stab wound. 'On more detailed examination,' he said, 'I found a large clot in the right lung.'

Martha interrupted. 'In your opinion was this a direct result of the assault on Roger Gough?'

Mark Sullivan looked squarely at her and not for the first time she thought what a waste – an intelligent man with clear blue eyes. He gave her a tentative smile. 'A pulmonary embolus or clot on the lung is a recognised complication of a stab wound to the chest,' he said. 'While it is noted in otherwise healthy individuals, particularly following air travel or in smokers, it would be most unusual for this to happen in an otherwise healthy youth. I can only conclude, therefore, that Roger Gough's death was as a direct result of the assault which had taken place a few days earlier.'

'Thank you.'

Martha drew in a deep breath. She had expected nothing else but...

She addressed the Goughs next. 'Before I pronounce the result of this court,' she said, 'you have the opportunity to speak about your son or to elect a friend or two to pay some tribute.'

Christina Gough turned in her seat to speak to someone behind her. Martha had hardly recognised Katie Ashbourne in her deep black, her hair closing like a curtain around her face. She stood up resolutely, teetered in a pair of black, high-heeled boots towards the witness box, faltered when her eyes rested on the Bible and looked up at Martha.

Martha felt a faint pricking of unease. Surely the girl would not recognise her?

Apparently not.

'You don't have to take the oath,' Martha said gently. 'You're not called as a witness but as a friend of Roger Gough's. Just speak up.' She gave the girl an encouraging smile.

Katie Ashbourne tossed her hair away from her face, fixed her eyes on the back row of the gallery and spoke in a high-pitched, nervous sounding voice.

'I was Roger's girlfriend,' she said, reading from a scrap of paper. 'We was going out for more than a year.' Her dark eyes scanned the room defiantly, as though she was challenging each and every single person there to contradict her. 'He was a gentle soul who wouldn't have hurt anybody. He was always kind to weak people and very fond of his mum and dad and little brother. Everyone liked him at school. He didn't have no enemies except the one. And that was enough. I can't think about nothin' since he died. Life isn't the same. I'll never forget 'im.'

Her eyes flicked across towards Martha and Martha nodded and made an attempt at a smile.

This wasn't the truth and she knew it. A month – a year – two years even. But Roger Gough would ultimately fade from her memory.

A boy was next in the witness box, a large, lumbering lad of thirteen or so who identified himself as Dave Arrett. He was wearing school uniform, maroon blazer, charcoal grey trousers, black shoes, apart from the black tie. He mumbled his tribute to his friend, that Gough had been the best friend he could ever have wanted, that Gough was true and loyal and...

Dave Arrett looked at no one as he stumbled over his words but as he stepped down from the witness box he must have caught Billy Gough's eye because he gave a nod and a smile and sat down, still smiling.

At the back of the court Shelley Hughes slipped in, almost unnoticed.

Martha watched Gough's loyal friend take his seat again and to her surprise Chelsea Arnold stood up, looking tinier and more vulnerable than ever. Martha noticed that she was wearing flat shoes like small ballet pumps with elastic criss-crossed at the ankle.

'Can I say something?' she said.

There was a mixture of emotion around the court, fury from Katie, confusion from the Gough parents, admiration from Gough's loyal school friend.

'Of course,' she said. 'But you must come to the witness box.'

No one in the entire court could have thought anything but that this was a great act of bravery from this child. What puzzled Martha was why she had chosen to speak out. And what was she about to say? Gough had plenty of other friends to speak out for him – an entire gang of them. So why Chelsea? Then it hit her.

Of course. It was part of her punishment for not being one of Gough's followers, for having befriended Callum. Perhaps she thought that doing this would buy her some peace and safety in her school.

The girl's throat was dry and constricted. She was having trouble getting her words out. Jericho kindly handed her a glass of water and she drank it noisily, like a greedy child taking milk. She cleared her throat, gulped, coughed, glanced at Martha – and spoke.

'I was asked to come here,' she said, 'to speak up for one of my class mates. But I've lost two people. Not just the one.' She too glanced around the courtroom until she found Shelley Hughes who was watching her with a deep frown, sitting slightly forward in her seat, her eyes fixed on the small girl.

'Roger Gough was a bully,' she said clearly. 'He made Call's life absolute hell. DreadNought 'ad it coming. I wasn't supposed to say this but I have now and I'm glad.'

She stepped down daintily from the witness box, looked at no one and walked straight out of the door leaving behind a scene of utter amazement.

Billy Gough's face was puce with anger. He'd left his seat and stood in front of Martha. 'You should have stopped this,' he said. 'It's a farce. Lies. That's all.' He wheeled round on his feet to face the watching rim of faces. 'She's a liar, that girl. A liar from a family of liars. It isn't true about my boy. It isn't true.' And to everyone's shock he put his hands in front of his face and gave one great, racking sob.

His wife, on the other hand, was still sitting, her face white and very angry. She looked at no one. But, watching her, Martha knew something was going on inside her head. Christine Gough gnawed her lip, pressed her fingers together, muttered something inaudible. Martha shivered. A witch's incantation? A hex?

Do we ever stop believing in these things?

Maybe not.

Martha risked a peep at Shelley Hughes. For the first time since they had met Shelley was smiling. She put her fingers up to her lips almost kissing them in a Papal benediction, then tilted them away, in the direction of the girl. A tribute to the girl who had, so bravely, spoken the truth when no one else would.

Martha waited for the furore to die down, watched as the skinny young journalist followed Chelsea out of the door and felt a glimmer of optimism that the true story behind the two deaths would see the light of a morning newspaper.

She cleared her throat and the whispering died down. 'The court finds that the death of Roger Gough on Friday the 16th of September at the Royal Shrewsbury Hospital was as a direct result of the injury inflicted on him on Tuesday the 6th of September by Callum Hughes outside Hallow's Lane School. The cause of death is thus clearly homicide,' she finished, listening to the sounds of Gough's parents' relief, the exhaled air and the quiet, *Thank God.* Billy put his arm around his wife and she dropped her head down on his shoulder.

It seemed an act of finality but Martha feared that this was only the beginning.

CHAPTER FIFTEEN

Martha left the court feeling drained by the Goughs. Inquests sometimes did this to her. Grief she could deal with. It was, after all, part of the job. But there was something vindictive and vengeful about their sorrow that concerned her.

And something in her feared for the gentle Chelsea. She felt apprehensive for the girl, almost as though she knew there would be reprisals. Callum Hughes might be beyond their vindictiveness. But she couldn't rid herself of the conviction that their emotions would turn into something tangible – as Callum Hughes's anxiety had changed, into murder and then into suicide. The Goughs patently felt real hatred for Shelley Hughes. Martha had seen them push into her outside the courtroom, shoving her out of the way with a real viciousness. And yet it had been Gough who had set off the chain of events.

So Martha had returned to the office with Jericho in reflective mood.

Where would all this vitriol lead? What could stem the flow of poison? And what could she do about it?

The mood hung over her like a pall of funereal smoke. She felt apprehensive and found it hard to concentrate all afternoon.

Her frame of mind was not lifted by a sudden, heavy

downpour and like many citizens of Shrewsbury she pictured the River Severn swirling and eddying while its level stole higher, and yet higher, to touch the arches of both English and Welsh Bridges, to wash out the town and cut it off as it had done on countless occasions.

The river had claimed a recent victim; the Floating Thai Restaurant – abandoned by its owners and now listing badly to one side. Some wag had repainted its name on the side – Thai-tanic. It had raised many a smile from the citizens of Shrewsbury as they caught the pun.

By five o'clock she felt she could not work any more that day and stopped off at Tesco's to buy some fresh salmon. She wanted to cook tonight, spend the evening with Agnetha and Sukey on the sofa, ring Sam and have something approaching a conversation with him, invite hers and Martin's parents for the weekend.

Have a life. Away from death.

But she had forgotten about Finton Cley coming over that evening to look at the antiques she was considering selling.

He arrived just as she was serving up dinner. New potatoes, steamed salmon steaks, homemade Hollandaise sauce and courgettes. For a moment she was confused by the doorbell ringing. Then she remembered.

He was a charismatic character with his curling hair, much too long for current fashion, the one, pirate earring, swinging in his earlobe. He was leaning against the side of the portico, grinning. 'You'd forgotten I was coming, hadn't you, Martha Gunn?'

It was useless to deny it. She laughed. 'Yes. I had, as a matter of fact. Sorry.'

'That's all right – so long as I can still take a look at your little titbits.'

'Yes. Of course. We were just eating. There's a little left over, Mr Cley. Would you like some?'

'Depends what it is.'

He was, she decided, insufferably arrogant.

'Well now,' she said, walking ahead of him into the kitchen, 'I don't know what to say. What if you reject my own, home cooking, Mr Cley?'

She could smell him. Tobacco, some exotic spice and, reassuringly, shampoo. Soapy and clean.

'Home cooking,' he said, settling into the spare chair and appraising Agnetha and Sukey very coolly, 'I never refuse.'

Sukey and Agnetha were signalling to each other in eyebrow semaphore. *Who is this guy?*

Martha put a plateful of food in front of Finton Cley and sat down, opposite him.

'This is Mr Cley,' she said. 'He has an antiques shop in town. I asked him to come tonight to look at some of the pieces in your father's study, Sukey. I thought I'd sell them before we decorate.'

'This,' she said to Finton, ' is my daughter Sukey and her au pair, Agnetha. As you can probably guess Agnetha is from Sweden.'

Finton Cley treated them both to one of the wide smiles which transformed his face from leering pirate to perfect gentleman. 'Charmed, I'm sure,' he said.

Agnetha giggled. 'Likewise, Mr Cley.'

But Sukey simply stared. 'So what are you selling, Mum?'

'Well I don't know, Sukes. It all depends on what Mr Cley offers me.'

The arch reply seemed to reassure her daughter and Sukey continued eating although Agnetha forked some salmon into her mouth and frowned. 'So tell me, Mr Cley,' she said, 'is the antiques trade still profitable or is it like many other businesses these days, much work with very little reward?'

'Is that a comment on your present situation?' Cley spoke with a mouthful of courgette.

'Certainly not. I was simply being curious. That is all.'

'It comes and goes,' Cley said casually.

Agnetha stretched across the table. 'Would you like some more vegetables?'

Cley's eyes focused on her engagement ring. He looked at it, at her, at it again and said nothing but took a spoonful of potatoes and one of courgettes. Sukey watched him with a mixture of curiosity and incredulity. Then, very deliberately, she stretched out her hand for some more vegetables too.

After supper Martha offered Cley a coffee but he declined. 'Keeps me awake,' he said.

'Then a beer?'

'That would be nice, Martha Gunn.'

Martha fished around in the fridge and pulled out a couple of lagers. She felt like one herself although she virtually never touched the stuff. Time to break the rules.

She handed him one then led him into the study and watched his response to the antiques as she showed him them, one by one. As she'd guessed he scrutinised everything, tipping the library table upside down, shining a light into the crevices, fingering the carvings. As he worked she watched him. How old was he? Late twenties, very early thirties at the most. Well educated but liked to pretend he was a ruffian. Yet at a guess he was familiar with Hardy and Tolstoy, Tennyson and Byron, Mozart and Beethoven.

When he crossed the room he suddenly turned and saw her watching him and she felt embarrassed. But to explain anything would be awkward, simply focus on the very thing she was avoiding. He would interpret her interest the wrong way. But she didn't fancy him. She was simply curious about him. That was all. She felt a compulsion to know more about him. Just a little more.

'Do you have a partner in your shop?'

He turned, giving her that mocking smile, as though he knew more about her than she could possibly know about him. 'Not really,' he said, speaking easily, dissolving the awkwardness she had *imagined*? 'My sister helps me now and then.'

'Not full time?'

'She can't do *anything* full time.' But the words were spoken without malice.

'Don't you find it hard, trying to buy as well as sell?'

'No, Martha Gunn,' he said, digging his hands into the pocket of his grey cargo pants, pulling out a tape measure and measuring up the width of the secretaire with a neat flourish which told her how many times he must have done this before. 'The stuff tends to come to me.'

Studying the glint in his eye and recalling the scent of marijuana which pervaded the inside of his shop she wondered exactly what stuff he was talking about but she let the matter ride.

Cley opened the secretaire and studied its interior before closing it and sliding it shut. Then he wandered across to the two chairs. 'Nice,' he commented. 'I love the deep buttoning. And leather's very 'in' at the moment.' His head swivelled round so she caught the full force of his very clear eyes. 'What period did you think they were?'

'Early Victorian, late Regency,' she ventured.

'Well – do you want me to give you individual prices or one for the lot?'

'The lot,' she said firmly.

He scanned the four pieces, silently working out their worth. 'Will four thousand suit, Martha Gunn?'

'Four thousand will suit very well.' In fact it was about what she had anticipated.

He laughed and shook her hand. 'If it suits that well,' he said, 'maybe I should have offered less.'

'Then I wouldn't take it.'

He nodded and she knew he was appraising her. There was a brief pause between them before Martha spoke. 'Another lager, Mr Cley?'

'That would be nice,' he said, 'though a glass of Rioja would be nicer.'

'You can have both the furniture and the glass of Rioja if you'll answer me a question.'

His eyebrows lifted. She disappeared into the kitchen, returning with an opened bottle of wine and two wine glasses. She filled them both, handed one to him and they settled down in the leather armchairs, opposite one another. Finton Cley was watching her warily over the rim of his glass. But she was in no hurry. She took a sip or two then spoke.

'Why do you always smirk when you say my name? Why do you always call me *Martha Gunn*, as though it has some significance?'

He sipped his wine too and made a pleased face. He looked suddenly smug, a public schoolboy who has just achieved top marks. 'I can't believe you've lived all your life and don't recognise your own name.'

'No I don't,' she said waspishly. 'So are you going to tell me?'

"'To Brighton came he
Came George III's son
To be dipped in the sea
By famed Martha Gunn.'"

'What?'

'Or do you prefer:

"There's plenty of dippers and jokers
And saltwater rigs for your fun
The King of them all is 'Old Smoaker'
The Queen of them 'Old Martha Gunn'
The ladies walk out in the morn,
To taste of the saltwater breeze,
They ask if the water is warm,
Says Martha, 'Yes if you please'."'

'She was a Brighton bathing attendant,' Cley said, his eyes twinkling with fun, 'and reputed to have attended the Prince of Wales. The Staffordshire Potters made a female Toby jug of her. There's one in Hanley museum, if you've a mind to go and take a look.'

'Really?'

He nodded. 'Don't tell me your parents didn't know this when they named you?'

'I don't know. I'll have to ask them, won't I?'

'Indeed you will. The good lady is portrayed with a hat bearing the three plumes of the Prince of Wales. She was quite a character by all accounts and died in 1815, aged eighty-eight years which is a goodly age, for the time, don't you think?'

Martha nodded.

'She's buried in St Nicholas's Churchyard, Brighton. You ought to take a trip down there and pay tribute.'

'I should. You're right.'

She leaned forward. 'More wine?'

He shook his head reluctantly. 'Driving, I'm afraid. And my business would soon go downhill if I couldn't get round. I'll send someone over tomorrow in a van to pick up the pieces – if that's all right, Martha Gunn?'

They both laughed and Cley gave a rueful glance. 'It isn't the same now you're in on the secret. What time shall the van come?'

'Ten-ish?'

'Ten it is.' He stood up and she saw him to the door.

The evening was chilly now with a wind blowing through the trees, making the leaves whisper and conspire. Martha watched the tail lights of Cley's Volvo disappear down the drive then stood for a moment.

It was so quiet here, so very very quiet.

After a moment more she turned around and went back inside.

CHAPTER SIXTEEN

It was Jericho who told her as she arrived late at work on the Wednesday. For some unknown reason the alarm had failed to wake either herself, Agnetha or Sukey and the morning had begun with pandemonium, all of them skittering to their bathrooms, throwing on clothes and eating toast in the cars on the way to work and school. Bobby's morning walk had been neglected; he was not a forgiving dog and glowered at her from the basket when she apologised and left his lead hanging on the back of the laundry door.

Jericho was waiting for her in the hallway, his face grave and she felt her heart sink. He often had to impart bad news to her over the telephone but when he considered the news was particularly bad he took it upon himself to wait for a face to face encounter. And he always looked like this, mournful, lugubrious eyes, his mouth drooping down and his hair, which always reminded her of Dickens's Scrooge – straggly and grey, looking even more so. So when she burst in, an apology ready on her lips, and saw he was standing in front of his desk (his particular position), with his face twisted into something more extreme than his habitual grave expression, she was alarmed and forewarned.

'Jericho? What is it?'

Her mind fled through all sorts of eventualities, his wife ill – dying – an accident to Agnetha, Sukey – 'Say something,' she said. 'You're frightening me.'

'Nothing to do with your family, Ma'am,' he reassured her quickly. 'Or mine, thank God.'

But his face was distorted with something.

'Then what is it?'

'Another nasty incident, Ma'am. To do with that poor boy's death, I'm sure.'

'What?'

'You might not have heard it but there was a house fire last night,' he said. 'Along Old Potts Way. A council house. A semi.'

'And?' She was feeling cold inside.

'There was a family inside. A young girl, her little baby brother. She was babysitting while her parents went up the pub with some friends.'

'Who was the girl?'

'Little Chelsea.' His eyes seemed to change. 'She's dead, Ma'am. Died at the scene they say.'

The image flitted through her mind, like a child ghost in a spooky, scary movie – only this was much much scarier. Real life and the depths to which human hope and despair, hatred and revenge can plummet, far below the earth's crust. Below any creeping, crawling creatures. Below the ocean's bed and the inhabitants of slime. Below any depravity known to any other creature in God's universe but man. An evil plotting, a deliberate destruction of a human body, together with its heart and soul.

Don't tell me this was an accidental fire. This is a consequence. A terrible consequence.

'And the baby?'

'Nine months old, Ma'am. Fighting for his life. They flew him to Birmingham. He's on life support. But I've heard the chances aren't good.'

A volcanic fury bubbled inside her. She was so angry she could have screamed with it. Instead she said dully, 'Get Inspector Randall on the phone, will you.'

And Jericho melted away.

She stood very still in her room, conscious of the diminutive figure flitting in front of her eyes with those neat movements, as elegant as a ballet dancer, the small pumps with their dainty straps criss-crossing over the feet, furthering the image. She tried to blink but stubbornly they continued to tap-tap out their rhythm. Until her phone bleeped and she picked it up, knowing who it would be.

'Alex?'

'Hello.' Even in the tersest of greetings she knew he felt as she did.

Angry.

'Alex, we have to stop this.'

'You're making some assumptions, aren't you, Martha?'

'Yes. I am. And so will you. Coincidence I can take, Alex, but this is screaming at us.'

It was the many-headed hydra. Cut one off and two appear. Crimes proliferate.

'Yes.' There was a pause before he spoke again, only to say, 'I should take you over there. You should see the scene.'

'Yep.'

'Half an hour? I'll pick you up.'

* * *

Robertson Way is a wide, fast road which runs between Monkmoor and the Lord Hill Momunment. In spring it is lined with a million daffodils and some small allotments. But either side are housing estates, some modern, some older, some detached, others semis. There are a few remaining council houses and privately owned residences. Chelsea had lived in one of the council houses.

It was easy to pick out the scene of the girl's death. Besides the official cars, police, fire service, the Gas Board, so many people had gathered – some on official business: TV reporters, cameras on shoulders, orange-faced people talking into arc lights, radio reporters, wafting huge furry grey microphones and the inevitable clusters of self-conscious voyeurs. All the way along the hedge at the front of the property was displayed the nicer side of human nature. Rows and rows of bunches of flowers, cellophane-wrapped, most with damp, fluttering messages of sympathy, love and the usual eternal question – why? – which always surfaces after tragedies like these – Dunblane, London tubes, senseless murders like this one.

They climbed out of the car.

The house had suffered badly when set on fire. The windows had cracked and blackened. Soot marked the spots where the flames had raged, splitting the glass. The fire service had wreaked its own damage, doors kicked through and water. Plenty of water.

And yet around the site of mayhem there were marks of normality.

The Ashbournes had been house-proud. The garden had been neatly tended. A small, white-painted wicket gate led into a newly laid cobbled path which neatly divided the front lawn. Influence of Charlie Dimmock, no doubt. But at the path's end normality ended. The front door was burned and splintered, inside Martha glimpsed yellow-hatted fire-fighters and uniformed police. They passed through to witness the havoc the fire had caused. The house had been destroyed. Nothing remained except charred rafters, melted shapes which must once have been furniture, the wires of a television. What the fire had spared, the water had completed the damage. The carpets were sodden. And the smell intense. It reminded Martha of the morning after a Guy Fawkes bonfire. The team of Scenes of Crime personnel was talking to the fire-fighters, watched by one police officer in a fluorescent green jacket. She listened in.

'The source of the fire was near the back door.' They all trooped through, into the kitchen or what had once been a kitchen. Now it was a soggy, burnt mess of chipboard and more melted plastic. Martha could see a collection of spice jars, cracked and blackened, cutlery, cracked china and what she guessed had probably once been a microwave oven.

'A hole was cut in the glass and petrol poured through.' The fire officer was including her in his tour. His eyes were cornflower blue and he had a serious, craggy face. He reminded her of Steve McQueen in *The Towering Inferno*. Same grim perception of fire, not as a source of warmth or to cook food with but as a ruthless, destructive force capable of distributing death, taking the lives of the most innocent.

The cornflower blue eyes met hers and she nodded a greeting.

He would know who she was. They had met, briefly, before.

'Once practically anything gets hot it's combustible,' he said. Pairs of eyes roamed the room and they nodded. 'Chipboard kitchen units, plastic tops, just bonfire food. The fire spread vertically.' He pointed upwards. 'Straight up, right into the girl's bedroom. It would have been fearsome within minutes. Hot gases, toxic smoke. The little boy was in the front bedroom and was a bit more lucky.' His face tightened. 'We hope. By the time the parents rounded the corner from their local it was way too late. And yet it had probably been burning for less than twenty minutes.'

Alex spoke in her ear. 'She made a couple of calls to friends from her mobile at just after ten. Neighbours saw the lights on downstairs at a quarter to eleven. They were switched off before eleven. By twenty past the Ashbournes were on their way home.'

Martha turned to leave. She felt queasy now as well as angry. But Alex was standing right behind her. 'I've seen enough,' she said in a low voice.

Once they were outside she faced him. He was an honest man. His revulsion would surely be as deep as hers. 'It's enough. This horrid proliferation must come to an end. We must flush it all out, clean the Augean stables.' Her hand pointed behind her. 'Have you any idea who committed this – this carnage?'

Alex's face was as grim as the fire officer's. 'We've got some ideas,' he said. 'Getting proof is going to be a different kettle of fish.'

'DreadNought's gang.'

He nodded. 'The Gough family have some very dangerous

contacts. This wasn't a schoolboy prank that went wrong. They watched and timed, laid their trap. Petrol isn't that easy to use.

'Then we have to return to the beginning, 'to the initial bullying, to the crime of Callum's assault on Roger Gough. Until we work our way through that we won't solve either Callum's death or this.'

'And how do you suggest we start?'

'Go to the school, Alex. Lay the bullying right open. Get statements. Confidential, if you like but get them. Make a statement that the murder of Roger Gough was a consequence. Only then can you concentrate on Callum's death.'

'Why would we need to? He hanged himself.'

She stared past him, at an ordinary street, in an ordinary town in middle England and felt an electric shudder. 'Are you *sure* of that?'

He stared at her. '*Aren't you?*'

'No.'

His face seemed to sink into tiredness. 'Neither am I. It's all too pat. Too...' Neither of them had the appropriate words to hand.

'Alex,' she said softly. 'If Callum didn't commit suicide where does it leave us?'

'Floundering,' he said.

'But how?'

'Send some officers to the school but you go to the prison, Alex. There's something there,' she said. 'Back there. The entire story must come out. We have to expose it all,' she said, 'from the first, to do justice to the dead.'

'We have several officers working on this case,' he said, his eyes drifting back towards the house. 'We expect early arrests over this, so if what you want is an exposé you'll have to point me in the right direction.'

'Tyrone Smith,' she said, 'would seem an obvious choice. And he hasn't got the brains to realise that you can only suspect. And then there are the prison officers.'

'So how do you think he died?'

'I have an idea,' she said. 'I think I read something somewhere. It's lurking at the back of my mind. Something to do with the hanging. No.' She put her hand on his arm. 'It isn't fair to say *anything* until I'm more sure. I'll speak to Mark and then I'll get back in touch with you.'

Alex was scowling. He looked over his shoulder as he drove away. 'Don't leave it too long, Martha.'

She glanced across at him. He had a troubled look which she hadn't seen before. 'Why?'

'I've just got a really bad feeling.'

'About things in general?'

'No.' He took his eyes off the road. 'Shelley Hughes, to be specific.'

She waited for him to enlarge.

'The vengeance of the Gough family is boundless,' he said. 'Roger Gough got his bullying nature from his parents all right. And Shelley Hughes will be a natural target for them.' He swung out onto the bypass. 'I wonder where all this will end up,' he said softly.

When they arrived at her office he opened the door for her but stood still, chewing his lip. 'One particular friend of the Gough family is a psychopath. He's been inside for three years for a really brutal assault on a night club owner who owed him some money. He did all sorts of things, Martha, including slicing off the man's nose. He's an absolute—' He managed a smile. 'Actually there isn't a word to describe him. We try to keep an eye on him but he slips around, turns up for his parole officer's appointments then vanishes back into the woodwork. He was seen having a drink with the Goughs at the local. He's the sort of guy who'd do it for nothing, just cause he'd enjoy the job. We can't be everywhere, watching him, sorting this mess, and protecting Shelley Hughes.' His brow was wrinkled with worry. 'We just can't do it.' She knew what he meant.

She nodded and took a couple of paces towards her door but he was beside her. 'Any more messages for Martha?' he asked lightly?

'No. My communicator has fallen silent,' she said. 'Alex – when this is all over promise me you will help me find out who is sending me the messages.'

'You realise it'll mean delving right back in your past?'

She nodded.

'I'm prepared for that but I have to know. Sometimes it feels like a threat – at other times it feels almost as if it's from a friend. I alternate between fright and curiosity but at some point I have to know. I want you to help me.'

'OK,' he said.

'Promise?'

'I promise,' he said.

And even that made her feel easier.

They parted then and immediately she was back in her own office she dialled the number of the mortuary to speak to Mark Sullivan.

He listened carefully to her questions, taking his time to answer each one fully.

And by the end of the conversation she was satisfied.

The difficulty would be to prove it.

Policemen are not pathologists and pathologists are not policemen. Each skill is incomplete in a murder case without the other. They must work hand in glove and find it possible to agree on the final scenario. And then they must present it to the satisfaction of a court of law. When they both agreed maybe, just maybe, you had the solution.

CHAPTER SEVENTEEN

Alex got back to her two days later, calling at her office on an off-chance to show her some of the statements his officers had squeezed out of the school fellows of Callum Hughes, Roger Gough and Katie Ashbourne.

His face looked younger and he seemed happy as he leaned back in the armchair, his long legs sticking out in front of him. 'I've had real cooperation from the headmaster,' he said enthusiastically. 'I think young Chelsea's death has finally tipped the balance.' His eyes looked half sad. 'Her death is finally going to make a difference. He's going to call a special assembly to talk about the problem of bullying. He's setting up special teachers as bullying officers who are sworn to secrecy. I think he can really stamp it out.'

'And Shelley Hughes? Is she safe?'

'Not too sure there,' he said, his face clouding over. 'She's still getting some unwanted attention. Graffiti's been daubed on her house. "*A murderer lived here. You're next.*" Stuff like that. She's beginning to crack.'

Then unexpectedly he smiled, a shy, friendly grimace. 'One bonus seems to have come out of all this though. Do you remember the teacher who spoke up for Callum, Farthing? Adam Farthing. He's taken it on himself to become her protector, keeping an eye out for her.' He grinned again, unselfconsciously. 'I think they're becoming fairly close.'

'Good,' she said. 'I'm glad. I liked her.' She hesitated. 'And Smith?'

He sighed. 'I've tackled him about the sleep business,' he said. 'I've made it quite clear that I don't believe he slept all the way through but he's just stone-walling me. Looking blank and generally being unhelpful. Keeps saying over and over again that he doesn't know a thing and that he slept all night, like a baby.' He sighed. 'I can't budge him, Martha. He's completely immovable. He's learned his lines and he's sticking with them. I'm not getting anywhere with him.'

'What about the prison officers?'

Alex's pupils seemed to sharpen. 'They're a bit more tricky. They're very defensive. The real issue is that I've got no real idea of where I'm going. I keep asking them the same old questions, all about timing and who was asleep. The trouble is, Martha, if I say anything to them it sounds like an accusation. Now if I start accusing them of bending the truth as far as times go it soon sounds like I'm accusing them of something much more serious.' All of a sudden he lifted his eyes and looked deep into hers. 'You're going to have to give me a clue, Martha,' he said softly. 'There's something you know that you're not telling me. It is, I suspect, something medical. I think you've probably had a word with Mark Sullivan and he's confirmed what you'd suspected. Am I right?'

She nodded. 'I'm impressed,' she said. 'You've put your finger right on the button. I did know something. It was something I heard years ago – a sort of pathology legend, if you like. Some experiments were done in the mid-nineteenth century by a guy called Casper. He hanged cadavers, some fresh, others a couple of hours old, but none had died from asphyxiation. And then he compared post-mortem changes with people who had hanged themselves. I've no proof,' she said. 'I don't know anything and I don't know how you could obtain proof except through a statement. I only know that something could have happened – that it was theoretically possible. Not that it did happen.'

'Tell me, proof of what, Martha,' he begged, 'or this case is not ever going to be solved.'

'I want you to question Walton Pembroke and Stevie Matthews,' she said. 'Speak to them again and simply throw some doubt on the cause of Callum Hughes's death. Say the pathologist is voicing some doubts. They won't know for certain that Mark hasn't thought of something else. Say the whole suicide verdict is uncertain and that I'm voicing concern.'

Randall still looked dubious. 'But Martha...'

She took no notice. 'And then investigate Walton Pembroke,' she said. 'See if you can find a connection. Any connection – however tenuous with the Gough family. Come on, Alex,' she said impatiently. 'You don't need me to point you in the right direction. Bank accounts. Mobile phones.'

He was still observing her. 'I'm still not absolutely sure what you're getting at,' he said.

She sat very still, frowning, hardly meeting his eyes. 'I'm afraid,' she said.

'Of what? You think the prison guards murdered Callum? That the Goughs paid the two guards to kill him?'

'No-o,' she said. ''I believe that Callum was already dead when he was hanged,' she said. And then, 'Think about the two prison officers? One is a craggy, ancient thing who's near to retiring. But it's the other one that I'm interested in. Inexperienced, new on the job, naive. Oh – so naive. She believed what he told her. I think it was that terrible combination of the one manipulating the other. Remember the bruises on Callum's face, the one on his chest. She restrained him – badly. Incompetently. Callum was an asthmatic. And he simply stopped breathing because she was sitting on his chest. I believe that Walton Pembroke was the one who encouraged her to do it. But the terrible crime was making it appear that the boy had committed suicide. Once I'd realised that Casper's experiments had proved that the post-mortem findings when a body had been strung up two hours after death I had a different time frame. Then the other injuries all made sense.'

Randall's eyes narrowed but she ploughed on.

'The reason that the restraint was performed was, I suspect, that Pembroke took some money from someone to rough Hughes up while he was inside and that someone has to have been the Goughs. It was no coincidence that Callum was put in a cell with the nastiest piece of work in the entire prison. It's obvious Walton Pembroke was waiting for him. It must have supplemented his pension nicely, taking the odd backhander from people. Looking after them – one way or another. This has got to be stopped and the only way to do it is to show the whole thing for what it was.

Alex's face was grim, his jaw set.

Martha ploughed on. 'I want to hold a joint inquest,' she said, 'on all three youngsters because they are cause and effect. Had DreadNought not laid into Callum Hughes both he and Callum would still be alive. So would Chelsea. If the entire thing had been stopped much earlier there would have been no deaths. Roger, Callum and Chelsea would have had lives. I firmly believe this, Alex.'

He read the determination in her face, the set of her jaw. 'We need a confession then.'

She nodded.

'Over to you,' she said lightly.

He stood up slowly. 'I'll be in touch,' he said.

But at the door he turned around. 'You want to be in on the questioning, don't you?'

She couldn't deny it.

CHAPTER EIGHTEEN

She felt nervous as she watched Walton Pembroke file in to the interview room. It was one thing to have an idea, another completely, to watch whether that idea could be true. Martha frowned. But if she was right...

Alex had rigged up CCTV so she could watch from another room, as well as pick up the sounds.

Pembroke had a confident, cocky air as he sat down, waiting as Alex Randall opened the questioning, checking names, times, places. It was a ruse, Martha knew, to put the suspect at his ease.

Then, quite abruptly, he turned the tables around. 'You knew the Gough family?'

Pembroke looked surprised and instantly wary. 'No,' he said gruffly. 'Why do you think that?'

Alex deliberately didn't answer but carried on. 'Someone rang you, did they, to tell you what had happened?'

Pembroke frowned. He didn't quite know how to answer. After a pause, he said, 'I had advance warning from Monkmoor Police Station that we would be receiving him, yes.'

Alex fixed his eyes steadily on Pembroke's face and left a pause.

Maybe he had rigged this too. Another police officer entered the room handing Randall a sheaf of papers. He scanned them before looking over the top of them at Pembroke and nodding.

It riled Pembroke. 'What's that supposed to mean?'

Randall did not answer Pembroke's question. Instead he commented, 'Set up nicely for your retirement, Walton?'

It was not a question.

And the ruse was working. Pembroke was squirming in his seat, eyeing up the door as though wondering whether he could possibly make a dash for it. 'I've got a pension,' he said.

Martha watched intently.

'You get some nice little bonuses through your job, don't you, Walton?' With a suddenness that shocked even Martha, watching through the screen, Alex Randall scattered the sheaf of papers across the table. 'These are your bank statements, Pembroke. Plenty of little backhanders. Rough 'em up a bit, Walt, give 'em a few extra spliffs, coke, we'll make it worth your while, eh? And murder?'

This, at last, rattled the prison officer enough to make him talk. 'No,' he said. 'No. I never would do murder. I never would. I'm not a criminal. I just take advantage of my position. That's all. Nothing really criminal. I might have accepted a few gifts in exchange for the odd favour. Slip things in, make sure they were comfortable. That sort of thing. Nothing else. I swear.'

Alex leaned in across the table and spoke in a soft voice. 'Someone asked you to set Callum up in cell 101, didn't they, with Tyrone as a cell mate.'

'Yeah. Yeah. I admit that. But not the other.'

'Prove it.'

Something snapped inside the prison officer. He looked at the door, the window, the ceiling, put his hands in his pockets, finally laid them flat on the table.

'It wasn't me.'

'Go on,' Randall said.

Pembroke gulped in some air. 'It was Matthews,' he said. 'She was over excited restraining him.' His eyes flickered away. He knew what he was doing, shopping a colleague.

'And you didn't pull her off?'

Pembroke knew he was beaten then.

'We're going to want statements from you,' Alex said. 'The one thing you can do for us is to tell us exactly what happened between you and the Goughs. Understand?'

Pembroke didn't even think about it. He nodded and stared at the floor.

Two police officers ushered Pembroke out of the interview room, straight into custody and as Martha watched Stevie Matthews entered. She looked pale and beneath her eyes were dark shadows.

Still in her black, wool uniform trousers and white shirt she sat down in the chair, gulped for air.

'Tell me how it was.' Alex's voice was still soft and soothing. He would coax the truth out of her.

Stevie Matthews tucked a strand of hair behind her ear.

'He was hysterical,' she said, 'when we took him out of his cell. Screaming and going bonkers, breathing hard. We knew the place'd be in uproar if we let him carry on like that. Walt told me you have to come on 'em hard. Particularly at first. Show them right away who's boss, like. I didn't mean to do anything wrong or illegal. Just restrain him. But I must have been too hard on his chest. He started off kicking and making a fuss. Walton knocked him a bit.' She was quick to defend her colleague. 'Not hard. Nothing terrible'

Behind the screen Martha muttered. The facial bruising. The bruises on the boy's chest wall. No – they had not been hard. Merely unfortunate.

'He went quiet. And then I got off him.' Stevie's lips were dry, hardly moving as she spoke, almost as though she had returned to the scene, to the long, echoing corridors full of locked doors and frightened boys.

And this one boy.

'He didn't move,' she said. 'I knew then...'

'And Walton had the idea?'

'He went wild, saying stuff about his pension, about how I'd crapped things up for him. And then he suggested...' Her eyes flickered to the floor and Martha knew just how distasteful the girl had found the idea.

'We dragged him back in.' For the first time she smiled. 'Tyrone was out for the count, snoring like a huge elephant. We got some computer wire, knotted it around his neck, and dropped him. That was that. Walton said it would just be classed as a suicide in custody and that he could retire with his pension and I could get on with my career.'

She broke then, dropping her face into her hands with great, racking sobs. A tear dripped through her fingers. 'And now I'm done for, aren't I?'

CHAPTER NINETEEN

Even *she* felt nervous. It had been a risky decision. The Press had gathered, sensing that this would be a momentous inquest. She had refused all interviews, saying she would restrict all her comments to this one arena.

The court was packed. In the sea of faces she picked out some she recognised: Alex, in the front, Jericho to her side, Mark Sullivan, quiet and expectant like the rest. She saw the Goughs, surrounded by friends and family, picked out Shelley Hughes sitting as close as she could to Adam Farthing, a tight group of thirteen-year-olds, the centre of which was Katie Ashbourne.

And she seemed to see other faces too – Chelsea Arnold's tiny form, in her pink ballet shoes, Callum's anxious face, Roger Gough, standing at the back.

She took a deep breath, waited for silence.

And got it. From the minute she had entered the courtroom a hush had fallen inside the entire area. She felt as though the world watched with baited breath and was glad that today, for once, she *had* worn deepest black. A dress of thin wool, a fitted, waisted jacket over it, the large jet buttons firmly fastened. She wore high-heeled, plain black court shoes and filmy tan-coloured tights. She had used straighteners on her hair so it was better tamed than usual. This was a solemn affair.

The Goughs still looked angry, Shelley Hughes vulnerable and Chelsea Arnold's parents whom she had met only briefly looked shell-shocked.

It was time to speak.

'I have taken a very unusual step today,' she said clearly, 'of holding a joint inquest on three separate deaths which took place at three different locations on three different dates. I have taken the decision to hold an inquest on the three deaths together for a very good reason. And that is because they were irrevocably linked. They were – dependant on each other and each happened as a consequence of the others.

'Most of the evidence has already been heard in court and I have discussed my verdict already with the police who are in agreement with my decision.' She caught a swift nod from Alex. 'I don't want to cloud the issues by a plethora of police evidence because it will rob my point of its power. The first death was that of Callum Hughes who died in custody at a Young Offenders' Institute. What was he doing there?'

She had half expected the Goughs to speak but for once they sat stony silent and motionless, frozen in their seats.

Shelley Hughes also sat quite still, clinging to Farthing.

'Callum Hughes had been the victim of a prolonged bullying attack at his school,' Martha said without looking specifically at anyone. 'He was being consistently terrorised. And as sometimes happens in these cases he turned on his oppressor. He bought a knife, sharpened it, and set out to free himself in a well-documented and witnessed attack. He was taken into custody and placed in front of the courts who decided he should not remain at liberty. I have to tell you now that Callum did not commit suicide but died accidentally, as a result of an encounter in the prison. This will be the subject of further police investigation.'

Pens were scribbling furiously on pads. One or two reporters were texting into mobile phones. She ignored them all.

'In the days that followed, while Roger Gough lay dying in hospital, the police tried very hard to find out why the attack had taken place but none of Callum and Roger's schoolmates owned up to what had happened. So the police were unable to access the truth because the other youngsters were still too frightened of Roger Gough's gang. In fact, if anything, Roger's friends had an even stronger sense of loyalty towards their gang leader and felt increased outrage towards anyone who did not toe the line.

One person, however, did speak out and this poor girl paid for it with her life.'

Martha stared around the courtroom. 'This is the terrible consequence of bullying and violence. Three families have lost their children in tragic and unnecessary circumstances. My object in bringing their stories to light is to make every effort in my power to ensure that this same story is never repeated again. These deaths were futile.'

The reporters were scribbling furiously, Martha noted, with a degree of satisfaction.

She would see this through.

She paused.

The reporters looked up, pens poised.

'I am not at liberty to divulge all the details of exactly what happened in the Young Offenders' Institute as police enquiries and, almost certainly, criminal charges will result but the ultimate verdict on Callum Hughes's death will certainly not be suicide but homicide. Roger Gough too died as the result of a homicide. Which leads me to the third death. Again the police are making enquiries but it seems certain that Chelsea Arnold died as the result of an arson attack on her home.' She paused. 'I am sorry to tell you that her baby brother did not survive the attack either.'

She studied the rim of faces. 'And what has all this achieved? Nothing. Grief, unhappiness, loss. I see in front of me relatives whose lives have been shattered. There must be an end to it. These four deaths have achieved nothing. Unless,' she paused, 'unless it is to ensure that this type of situation does not happen again. Ever.

'We have three murders – three families who have all suffered. One family's loss is equal to another's. No one has benefited.' She fixed her eyes on the Goughs. 'No one has won. You have all lost.'

Martha leaned back in her seat.

'These,' she said, 'are the results of my findings.'

She waited for the watching people to absorb all that she had said before continuing.

'Callum Hughes was fond of war poetry. In particular the poems of Wilfred Owen. Part of the poignancy of this young man's death is that he died in November 1918. His parents could hear the Armistice bells ringing out in Shrewsbury when they received the news of his death. They must have grieved while others celebrated.'

She paused. 'I want to read you an excerpt from just one of

his poems. It's called 'Strange Meeting' and is an imagined encounter between a German soldier and a British Tommy.'

All eyes were on her.

"I am the enemy you killed, my friend.
I knew you in the dark: for so you frowned
Yesterday, through me as you jabbed and killed.
I parried; but my hands were loath and cold.
Let us sleep now..."

She allowed the words to sink in before adding softly, 'Let *them* sleep now.'

CHAPTER TWENTY

She had expected an aftermath – but nothing could have prepared her for the furore that broke out in the court. The Goughs, parents of the first victim, were taken into police custody before they reached the door. Outside journalists, friends, school-mates, all watched open-mouthed as Roger Gough's parents were bundled into the police van.

One fine morning six months later, Martha was working in her office when there was a knock and Jericho walked in. 'Detective Inspector Randall has rung,' he said. 'He wonders if he could possibly call on you.'

'Of course.' Like everyone else Martha had anxiously awaited the outcome of the police investigations.

Jericho left the door open and returned. 'He'll be along in half an hour,' he said, adding, 'shame about his wife.'

He lingered in the doorway.

Martha caved in. Jericho was an incorrigible gossip and would not be deflected once he had decided to speak. 'What about his wife?'

'In and out of mental hospitals,' he said. 'She's got bipolar disorder. No end of trouble she's caused him. Spending money like there's no tomorrow. She rang the paper, I heard, and accused him of all sorts of things. Going off with other women, stealing from their bank account. Poor man,' he said. 'It's come close to costing him his job.' He retreated before she could respond and closed the door deliberately and slowly behind him.

The knowledge of Alex's home circumstances made her look at him in a new light when he arrived twenty minutes later. He looked tired. She noticed the lines around his eyes, the hard set to his mouth. She could read the suffering there. She had always sensed it but until now, she had not understood it. Now she did. Once Jericho had bustled through with cups of coffee, eagerly and unashamedly eavesdropping in on the conversation, Alex began.

'You know, Martha,' he said, settling back in the chair, his long legs stretched out in front of him, 'one nice, predictable thing about villains is that they will all shop their fellows in exchange for a little plea bargaining. I'm almost awash with information. You wouldn't believe how many hours we've spent taking statements and ferreting out the ugly truth.'

He grinned at her, took a sip of his coffee. 'I almost don't know where to start.'

'Start with the Goughs.'

'Well, we've got them on a conspiracy to commit murder charge. As we thought Peter Bowman was the singularly unpleasant arsonist.' His mouth twisted. 'He charged the Goughs eight hundred pounds for setting fire to Chelsea's house. He's back inside and, I hope, will never come out. He's a wicked old lag who's been in and out of prison all his life. There's nothing he wouldn't do for a bit of money, which goes straight on whisky and cigarettes. He's done some long stretches but, somehow, we've never really managed to bang him up for life. They met up in one of the town pubs and a barmaid finally leaked details of their plans. She only heard bits but it's enough.'

'And the Goughs?'

Alex looked a little less certain. 'Well, they're bound to say that they were grief-stricken at Chelsea's speech in the court and they will get some sympathy. There's no doubt about that but I'd be very surprised – and disappointed – if they got less than ten years for their part both in the arson and the bribery of Walton Pembroke. Terrified of being on the receiving end of his own prison system he's really ready to croak.' He permitted himself a smile. 'My bet is that he won't be drawing that pension. Conspiracy to pervert the course of justice, concealment of a body, accepting bribes.'

'Will you be able to pin that on him?'

Alex looked less sure of himself. 'It's going to be very difficult to prove exactly what he did,' he said. 'The Crown Prosecution Service is choking on this one. However, we have a safety net. The Prison Officers' Union hold their own enquiries and they are more stringent than ours. Pembroke's currently out on bail, suspended from work and will not be going back to Stoke Heath. When we investigated his bank account we realised he'd had a roaring little trade, supplying drugs, roughing inmates up, making life a little smoother for those who had relatives willing to pay, even smuggling the odd woman in.'

'Stevie Matthews?' she prompted.

'Unlawful killing, perverting the course of justice but no

jury is going to believe she acted out of malice or alone. It's obvious that Pembroke was the real villain. He was experienced enough to know that her restraint, on a terrified asthmatic, could have killed him and I always felt that making sure Callum was out of sight of the CCTV was a deliberate action.'

'So what about the school?'

'Put it like this,' he said with a smile, 'things have got a lot better not only at Hallow's Lane but at other schools in Shrewsbury. This case has focused attention on the problem. I've been asked to provide officers to visit classrooms and speak to the pupils, even to look at playgrounds and advise on reducing the number of dark areas where assaults can take place. All the officers I've sent in have reported a real determination to make schools safer and stamp out bullying.'

'That's good.'

He was silent for a moment. 'I'll tell you something that's been puzzling me.'

'Yes?'

'How did you know that Callum hadn't killed himself?'

'I didn't, Alex, I suspected partly because I knew the post-mortem findings would be the same whether he had died from hanging or another cause and been strung up later to make it look like a suicide. I simply collected all the facts and laid them out in a row. When Shelley said that he was asthmatic I could see only too clearly that he easily could have asphyxiated from an over-zealous restraint. The terror could have caused bronchoconstriction and we know he was terrified. The videotape showed us his mental state only too clearly. Then again – Stevie Matthews was new on the job. It was very likely that apart from her initial training sessions she had never actually applied restraint in a practical situation. As I've mentioned there was the avoidance of the camera's eye. Pembroke had worked at Stoke Heath for years. Don't tell me he didn't know the exact location of every single CCTV camera. It was no coincidence that Callum was frogmarched out of sight. Then there were Callum's injuries, the marks on his chest and face. String all those facts together and it fitted into place just that bit too neatly. Casper simply pointed the way forward.'

Alex was smiling at her. Saying nothing. His face looked younger, softer. One wouldn't call him a handsome man but there was something craggy and masculine that made his an attractive face. Martha smiled back.

'There is one other thing.' He spoke quietly. 'I feel worried about your stalker. These incidences can escalate all too easily. I took the liberty of asking an offender profiler to examine the incidents you'd told me about and he feels that we should take it seriously. He also feels sure that the perpetrator is someone you've had professional dealings with. That's enough for me, Martha,' he continued. 'We'll need details of every case you've conducted since you came to Shrewsbury.'

'What? There must be thousands.'

'Only the ones where you've played an active part in the verdict,' he said.

'That does narrow the field a bit. But it must still be hundreds, Alex.'

Alex raised his eyebrows and Martha was silent. She had suspected this herself, that her job had led someone to home in on her. 'Then I'll organise Jericho,' she said finally.

Randall stood up then. 'Well, that's it, Martha.'

She stood up with him. 'Goodbye, Alex.'

He was gone and she sat back in her chair, thinking.

She still had her own ghosts to lay to rest, plenty to tackle yet in her life. Many cases of tragedy to deal with in the future but she would never forget these three lives which had been wasted so wantonly. Perhaps like the deaths in the First World War she should tell herself that all had not been in vain and that young lives had not been wasted without some benefit.

But in her heart of hearts she was not convinced.

She stood up and looked out of the window, straight across the town, at the spire of St Mary's, scene of the first hang gliding tragedy in 1739. What future deaths would she need to unravel? Which would Alex find had led to someone victimising her for more than a year? And what about her personal life? Was she destined to follow the example of Martha Dias, also buried at St Mary's?

Here lies the body of Martha Dias,
Who was always uneasy and not over pious.
She lived to the age of three score and ten,
And gave to the worms what she refused to the men.

Would that be her epitaph?

She sighed, felt vaguely and momentarily depressed then caught sight of her mobile phone flashing.

It was a text from Sam, simply hoping that she was 'all

right' and that 'Bobby was fine'. She smiled. No need for the mistletoe code.

So as usual, she must move on into her own personal and professional future, her two children at her side. She texted Sam back telling him they were all fine too.